# MURDER
# IN FALSE FACE

by George Childerness

**WILDSIDE PRESS**

# MURDER
# IN FALSE FACE

This book has been condensed slightly in order to cooperate with the war-time paper conservation plan of the War Production Board.

PRINTED IN U. S. A.

# CHAPTER 1

K ENT LOOKED UP from the menu and coughed. He said in a small voice, "Dear me, these prices are frightfully high." He ran his eye down the right-hand column. "You may bring me some tomato juice, ham and eggs, dry toast and a container—ah —I mean a cup of coffee."

I reached across and plucked the menu from his fingers. "Make that two steaks. Thick, rare ones, smothered in mushrooms. And while we're waiting snap up a couple of Sidecars."

Kent turned beet red. His eyes popped. He said sharply, "Boy!"

The man turned. Kent said in his most acid voice, "Change those Sidecars to Scotch and soda." He waved the waiter on, leaned back and gloated. He knew I hated Scotch. He opened his mouth.

I said hastily, "I know, I know. Newsprint is up a quarter of a cent a pound, circulation is off seven point four percent, and we're twenty-two columns down on advertising over the same period last year."

"Twenty-seven columns," he corrected.

I raised one shoulder in a hopeless gesture. "It's the end. Let's eat and be merry while we can."

He almost choked. He said, "Have the graciousness to cease tormenting me. The weakened condition of my first newspaper is no joking matter."

I attacked the steak put before me. "What did you expect after neglecting it for a year? You should have settled with Dillon in the first place. If the Free Press is in lousy shape today, it's your own fault."

Kent sniffed and wolfed his steak. I hadn't counted on it when I took the job, but part of my works as confidential assistant to this crackpot publisher of twenty-odd newspapers was to prevent him from starving himself to death on the grounds of economy and, incidentally, me along with him. My other duties were vague, including as they had, over a five-year tenure, stenography, reporting, killing snakes (Denver), subornation of perjury (Milwaukee) and grave robbery in a southern city which even now I do not care to name.

Kent growled, "There was more involved in the Dillon matter than mere financial consideration. A great newspaper cannot surrender meekly to libel suits."

"G'wan, you faker," I scoffed; "he had us dead to rights. We got off dirt cheap."

"Cheap!" Kent exploded. "God in heaven, do you call five thousand dollars cheap?"

I said plaintively, "For Pete's sake, will you quit moaning? You paid five thousand dollars to square a possibly nasty libel rap and sold twenty-five thousand dollars worth of extra papers, not to mention saving the taxpayers a cool half million. What more do you want?"

· Kent said with dignity, "I want justice."

I decided it was time to change the subject. "Let's go in the club rooms and take a whirl at Lady Luck. Hank says they have the classiest roulette layout in town."

Kent said dubiously, "You know my sentiments about gambling. However, I have always wanted to observe the functioning of these establishments. An hour should suffice to lose as much as you can afford and may furnish an interesting article on games of chance."

I thought, "Oh my God," but all I said was, "That's the spirit." I coughed. "Unfortunately I am somewhat broke at the moment. Advance me a hundred and I'll demonstrate exactly how it's done." I held out my hand.

"A hundred dollars!" he exploded. "You're insane. I might venture say five or ten, but a hundred—"

"Just as a start," I explained. "It's my money I'm asking for, isn't it?"

Kent paid the check, and flung his napkin on the table. He said, in a voice trembling with rage, "You confounded, impudent whelp, I ought to discharge you on the spot. A hundred dollars, indeed. Not even a hundred cents." He pushed back his chair. "If you can gamble on credit, you are at liberty to do so. I shall be at the office." He made a dignified exit.

I finished my coffee, then picked my way through the dining room. A tough-looking gent with bushy eyebrows and a dinner coat lounged against a door marked "Private Office." He shot me a look from under the eyebrows, then stood aside.

The door opened on a narrow corridor connecting with the adjoining building, whose entire ground floor was given over to gambling devices. I ignored the craps layout, birdcages, poker and faro. My dish is the wheel. I didn't especially feel like playing, but having put on an act to get away from Kent for a few hours, my conscience demanded I at least go through the motions. I bought a fifty-dollar stack of chips from a cashier who seemed surprised at so modest an investment. I watched a few spins, and when black showed three times running I put a dollar chip on the red for the next play.

The roulette table, with a seating capacity of twenty-five to thirty, was getting only a desultory play at so early an hour—a handful of seated customers really working at it and three or four idlers like myself tossing away a few dollars without even bothering to sit down.

A soft voice with a hint of a lisp in it said behind me, "Not giving us much of a play, are you?"

I glanced around at a small lean man, bandbox neat in a midnight blue dinner jacket. His lips were smiling, but his almost black eyes snapped with suspicion. Firelli. Nobody who had ever seen him, even for a few seconds, could fail to recognize him the second time. Firelli was sleek and black—black glistening hair and swarthy skin stretching tightly over high cheekbones, black eyebrows, and even a fuzz of curling black hair on the backs of his hands and powerful strangler's fingers. Firelli was as sleek and dark as a black panther and just as deadly.

I smiled back at him, and pointed to my small stack. I said, "Just killing time."

Firelli said intently, "You're Phelps—Kent's muscle—aren't you?"

I decided against taking offense. "Not muscle—secretary. I'm off tonight. This is on my own time. I didn't realize I was in one of your joints."

"When did you two get in?" Firelli persisted. "Wasn't you in Seattle?" He watched me narrowly.

I said with suddenly flaring temper, "What the hell is this—a cross-examination? If you don't want me in your crummy dive, come right out and say so."

He stood over me, hesitated, apparently decided against voicing whatever he had in mind, and walked off. He had a peculiar stiff-legged gait, half strut, half stalk. The short hairs of my neck tingled as I turned my attention to the table. Definitely, I smelled a taint in the wind.

The table began to fill up nicely. The play was faster, bets bigger. I ambled along on my fifty dollars well over an hour. Then two men slid into the vacant chairs alongside me and plumped down big stacks, mostly hundred dollar yellows. The croupier gave them a startled glance, mumbled over his shoulder to a page. The youngster listened, nodded, and sauntered off with no evidence of haste. I inspected the newcomers out of the corner of my eye. They were a hard-looking pair, big and muscular, with cold shoe-button eyes. Like me, they wore ordinary business suits.

The one at my side said affably, "If I win the first play, I'll buy a drink for luck." His words were addressed to me.

I said, "Why not? If you lose it's my treat."

He laughed and nudged his companion, who glanced at me briefly. The first one said, "Jerry Candle's the name."

The name meant nothing to me. I said, "Chet Phillips," and shook hands gravely.

Jerry said, "Pleased to meet you. Shake hands with my pal, Roy Meade."

I shook hands with Roy across Jerry. It was all very formal and proper.

Jerry flipped a hundred-dollar chip on the felt. It landed on two. Twenty-six showed—not even close.

I said, "My treat."

They made a few more plays without a hit. Our drinks came. So did three broad-shouldered young men, natty in midnight blue dinner coats. They stood behind our chairs, watching the game over our heads. They looked like trouble.

Roy hit an eight to one for a hundred dollars on his fifth play. He offered to let it ride.

The croupier shook his head. "Sorry. A hundred-dollar limit at this table."

One of the blues leaned over. He murmured, "There's a no-limit table upstairs, gentlemen."

The tip of Jerry's tongue showed between his teeth. He said, "Scram, cokey. You make me nervous." He started to rise.

Roy pulled him down. He said, "Cut it out, will you?" He appeared only moderately annoyed. He looked up at the blues. "You boys better blow," he advised. "My friend don't like people to stand behind him."

The blues exchanged glances, and moved a few feet down the table. Jerry said with heavy contempt, "These penny bank joints." He turned to me. "What's your racket, pal?"

"I'm a reporter, sort of."

He said, "No?" with awe. "You mean you put things in the papers?"

Roy said scornfully, "Of course he does." He carelessly flipped two hundred-dollar yellows on black. The croupier winced, looked to the blues for a cue. They stared stonily ahead. The bet went unchallenged. Black won. Roy said, "The hell with it. That's enough for a complimentary play. Let's go to the bar."

I seemed to be included. We went to the bar, sat down at one of the small tables flanking it. Jerry ordered a new round of drinks.

"What paper you with?" Roy asked.

I explained my status as Kent's secretary.

He frowned. "Didn't you guys put the blast on Firelli and that mouthpiece what's-his-name, about a year ago?"

I said such was indeed the case.

"Wait a minute." Roy's brow cleared. "It's coming back now. This lamebrain mouthpiece pulled some stuff for Firelli on a traction fix, and your sheet caught him off base. Yes or no?"

"Yes."

"Sure. You must be the muscle who put Joey Aces and Ringtail in the hospital."

I said warily, "Friends of yours?"

Roy said, "Our friends don't go to hospitals." He was amused. "How do you stand on a proposition?"

"Not a chance. I have a good job. I don't sleep regularly, but when I do it's on a bed, not a slab."

"For Christ's sake." Jerry sounded outraged. "What do you take us for, a couple of hoods?"

Roy drained his drink in two gulps. "This is a writing job we got in mind—needs a kid with guts," he persisted. "What we want is a bunch of writeups like your traction stuff, only about gambling and such."

I tilted my glass. "Where are these joints?"

Roy said, surprised, "Why, right here."

Jerry added his voice. "This is clean-up stuff, sure fire. We feed you the dope. All you do is sit wherever the hell you sit when you make up this scrap and grind it out as we chuck it to you."

"What about Firelli? He won't take it lying down."

Roy waved Firelli aside. "We'll tend to him. You write and leave Firelli to us." He lowered his voice. "Ten grand is in it."

I said, "You boys have the wrong slant. Even if I were willing to play along, I couldn't slip the stuff past our city editor, much less Mr. Kent."

Jerry nodded. He said, "No offense," and fingered the empty glass, yawned, and prepared to leave. "We'll see you around, pal."

We shook hands again. Roy paid for the drinks, insisted on ordering me another. They left.

I decided to take a final whirl at roulette, lose the chips I had and call it a night.

As I moved away from the table, what felt like a ton of fat rammed me head on. I saved myself from sprawling on the floor by some quick footwork. "Why don't you look where you're going?" I snarled. A good brawl suited my mood perfectly.

I followed a tremendous paunch up over an acre of white shirt, three pendulous chins, a raw red mouthful of stained teeth, sea-lion moustache, and didn't need the pock-marked face and bald mushroom of a head to know I had drawn a darb for a fight—none other than Police Commissioner Osmond.

I said, "Excuse me, Commissioner. I didn't see you in time." I started to detour around him.

He gripped my shoulder in a vise clasp. I knew better than to struggle. He said, "Well, by God, you sure are in a hurry, young feller." He peered at me through fat-bedded myopic eyes. I smiled and waited, hoping he wouldn't recognize me.

His companion, however, did. He was a pallid, wispy-moustached little man with bleached skin, thin yellow hair and the steadfast manner of a courageous rabbit. District Attorney Jason Hendrickson knew everybody and catalogued each person according to his capacity for potential use.

Hendrickson said, "Well, well, Mr. Phelps, is it not?" He gave me a tremulous smile. "And how is Mr. Kent?"

Phelps didn't mean a thing to Osmond, but Kent's name registered. He released my shoulder. He rasped, "That bastard. We got a criminal libel charge against him kicking around. Where is he?"

"Had a charge," Hendrickson corrected gently. "It was dropped some months ago, I believe."

"That's right. We settled." My shoulder ached. Loyalty prompted me to add, "We'd have licked Dillon easily if we had been willing to go into court and show the sources of our information."

Hendrickson struck an attitude. "Whenever a newspaper breaks the law it seeks refuge behind the freedom of the press concept. If the reforms I have suggested are adopted—"

"By God, do we jaw with this bastard all night?" Osmond interrupted. "I want a drink." He dragged Hendrickson to the bar. I kept on to the roulette table.

I won. Across the table, a blonde girl had also hit . As the ball landed in the number slot she gasped and looked up. I wasn't paying much attention, only caught her eyes for a moment before she lowered them again. They were the first friendly pair I had seen all evening.

While the wheel was spinning for the next play, a square-jawed lad came across the room and stood behind the girl's chair. He bent over, whispered in her ear. Annoyance flashed across her face, and she shook her head so that the long blonde hair rippled. She turned toward me, giving me a good closeup view of her face. It was the kind of face they drew for magazines like *Vogue*—there are no faces like it but there ought to be—long, with high cheekbones, sloping planes to the chin, eyes slanted and drawn down, mouth proud and cruel. I guessed it was mostly makeup.

I thought, What can I lose? I said across the table, "Mind if I follow your leads for a while? My hunches have been running terrible."

She smiled. "I'm not very lucky either, most of the time. But you're welcome to try." She had a deep, rich voice.

The lad behind her threw me a murderous look which I ignored. We each put a five-dollar chip on black, won, let it ride, won again.

I said with approval, "This is more like."

The lad bent over her again and talked urgently into her hair. She frowned, turned her shoulder, and said crossly, "Oh, go away."

I thought it time to take a hand. I moved around the table and took the empty seat. I said, "We need a drink," and she nodded. While I was spotting a page, the lad crossed over behind the girl. He said out of the corner of his mouth, "Beat it."

"Be your age," I advised. The girl giggled, highly amused by this bit of byplay. She put two fives on "Odds," and when I followed, our hands touched briefly. She smiled at me with nice teeth.

I said, "Cozy little place you have here."

"Yes, I'm thinking of building," she agreed. "What's your name?"

"Chet Phelps. I'm the Fuller Brush man."

"Oh no, you can't be. You didn't say ting-a-ling."

I said, "Ting-a-ling."

"That's better." She turned to the lad. "Don't sulk, honey. I've simply got to have a new hairbrush."

"Of course," he agreed. He put his hand on her arm. "Come on, let's get out of here and I'll buy you one." He sounded anxious.

She shrank from his touch. "And leave Chet? I couldn't do that. Besides, I'm ahead for the first time this week."

I said, "Perish the thought. I brought my samples." I gave the lad the eye. "Look, chum, the lady doesn't want you around."

He crashed his fist into my face before I could get up, a dirty trick. I kicked the chair out from under, sent it spinning away. A midnight blue came plowing over. I ducked under the lad's next swing and brought my heel down on his toe. When he came over forward I lifted my knee fast and gave him the elbow under the chin. He grunted and sprawled on the floor. The blue shouldered me aside, and jerked him to his feet with one hand. In the other he held a rubber sap which he repeatedly brought down on the kid's head.

I said, "Hey, you didn't need to do that."

The blue said shortly, "I didn't do nothing, mister. You go on with your play." He had the lad by the collar. He beckoned to another blue. Between them they lugged the kid away. The croupier shoved a pile of white chips across the table. I hadn't realized I had any money riding.

I turned to the blonde. I thought she would be boiling mad. I said, "I'm sorry. I didn't mean to hurt your friend."

She looked white and frightened. She said faintly, "I scarcely know him. He's one of those men who hang around here." She motioned me to sit down. "He's been annoying me all evening."

Our drinks arrived. So did a man in full evening clothes. He said, "Good evening, folks. What seems to be the trouble?"

I said, "No trouble at all. A little misunderstanding, but it's been cleared up nicely."

The croupier said, "Make your plays, ladies and gentlemen." Full-dress-suit watched for about a minute, then drifted away. I said to the girl, "It would help if you told me your name."

She smiled above her drink. "Gail Dillon."

I must have swallowed a mouthful the wrong way. She patted my shoulder solicitously. The croupier looked disgusted. I could see the blue across the room watching me carefully.

The Gail cocked her eyes at me. They were bright, mocking. Her lips were inviting, a trick of makeup, I suppose, but effective. I shoved ten dollars on an eight-to-one group. I said, "If it's a merry-go-round, let's stay on for another ride, Gail Dillon."

---

# CHAPTER 2

ONE MOMENT I was asleep, the next wide awake, though I hadn't opened my eyes. I was awake, hence alive, but only barely. Keeping my eyes shut, I touched my face. It felt numb.

I opened one eye, then shut it hastily as an impression of strange surroundings impinged on my retina. At the hotel my bed fronted a window; here I faced a blank wall. I thought, Take it easy, boy; everything will be all right. I listened for the familiar floor-shaking rumble of the presses always audible in the cubbyhole behind Kent's office.

Nothing. Yes, there was, too, the regular breathing of someone deep in sleep. In my present delicate condition it paid to be sure, so I held my own breath, but the sounds continued. Company in bed seemed roughly established.

There appeared to be no choice but to risk another look. The shock of certainty practically killed me. Merely by rotating my eyeballs, without moving my head, I knew I had never in my life seen the room. I carefully slid out of bed. I was wearing pajamas, gay striped ones of a pattern owned neither by Kent nor myself.

I padded around the bed to the other side. A mass of golden hair spilled over the pillow, half concealing a set of features. Bells began to ring in my mind. Gail Dillon. She slept with one bare arm over her head, a frown wrinkling her brow. Memory came flooding back—dinner with Kent, meeting the Gail over the roulette table at the Club Cabana, a fight, drinking. Here memory rang against a stone wall.

Even under the acid test of daylight, the Gail was a stunner. Heavy violet shadowed her eyes and her mouth drooped tiredly. She looked less sophisticated, more like a little girl, with her tousled hair and long lashes curling against her cheek.

A wave of dizziness hit me as the hangover took hold again. I tottered about, and finally located the bathroom. My haggard face in the mirror might have been another blow if I hadn't already been beyond sensation of any ordinary sort. A twinge in my left knee revealed I had scraped a good inch of skin from it in the course of what must have been a memorable night.

I fumbled in the cabinet above the sink, found it barren of first-aid supplies. There were towels in the rack, however. After I washed my face and cleaned my knee I felt a little better.

A new idea struck me. My trousers lay tossed on a chair near the bed. I tiptoed over and felt in the pockets. There were crumbled bills of respectable denominations jammed in loosely. Since I had started the evening with about eighty-five dollars, I certainly hadn't been slugged and rolled.

A quick glance at the bed showed the Gail still asleep. I shucked off the strange pajamas, climbed into my pants. I looked around for my shirt and, after a bit of hunting, found it practically under the bed. It was badly soiled. I was about to put it on anyway, when I noticed an open suitcase on the floor near a dresser. When I found it contained only feminine wear, I sighed with relief.

I straightened up. The conveniences provided for unexpected guests hadn't been exhausted after all, because there, on top of the dresser, was a new shirt, still fresh in its cellophane wrapper, and beside it a tie of conservative pattern, also new.

The shirt fit. My own taste runs to a neat white, while this was a solid blue. I made a mental note to take the matter up with the management, put on the tie, shoved my old shirt and tie into a pocket of my overcoat which I found tossed in a far corner.

Still in my bare feet but otherwise fully dressed, I made a swift search of the place, apparently a small apartment. Closets and dresser drawers were empty. The clothes the Gail had worn and her purse were on another chair close to her side of the bed. Outside of the shirt and tie, which may have been intended for me, I found no other male possessions. There was no phone.

I put on socks and shoes. Whatever explanation lay behind the apartment and my presence in it would have to await Gail's rising. And, I thought, if she felt even approximately the way I did, I had no intention of being in her line of vision when first she opened her eyes. No indeed.

A door led into a small kitchen, where I finally encountered signs of previous occupancy. A cupboard held a few dishes, cups and saucers and a paper sack half full of coffee. I located the percolator among pots in the stove compartment. A dinette table and two straight-backed benches were squeezed into a tiny alcove below the single window. I recognized the layout as typical of small furnished apartments in many parts of the city.

I washed the percolator, filled it with water and coffee, turned on the gas. I explored the refrigerator and found it bare, not even turned on. The Gail had better like her coffee black and without sugar.

I turned at the sound of steps. The Gail was leaning against the doorway. She had on a green negligee which did nice things for her figure. Her hair was loose about her face.

She flexed her arms and regarded me gravely. "Hello." Her eyes flicked to the coffee pot, over to the two places I had set at the table.

"Sit right down," I invited. "But you'll have to take it straight. I couldn't find sugar or cream."

She brushed by me and slipped into one of the bench seats. "You'll find sugar on the second shelf. I always take it black."

The sugar was where she indicated. The coffee looked about ready; I'm no expert in these matters. I poured two cups, took the opposite bench. The worst was over, I hoped. She hadn't been what you would call cordial, but neither had she hollered copper, which, in my present frame of mind, was enough.

I said, "Believe it or not, this is a new experience for me."

Her head was bent over the cup. I couldn't see her eyes, but the corners of her mouth twitched. She said, not looking up, "Spending a night with a strange man isn't exactly part of my routine either, Chet."

I must have looked pretty silly, because she suddenly lifted her head and smiled. I grinned, and the ice was broken.

I said ruefully, "Anyway, I'll bet it was quite a party while it lasted."

"It certainly must have been."

My jaw dropped. I said weakly, "Don't tell me you don't remember either?"

She nodded. "This is my apartment, though I don't use it very often, and I can't recall coming here." She evaded my eyes. "A girl has to have some place where she can get away from her family once in a while," she added defiantly.

"I know how it is." I felt the bulge in my pocket. "I have a lot more money than I started out with last night. Didn't we team up at the wheel and agree to split our profits?"

She said, "I have my share," and bit her lip.

"If you recall that much, maybe you can fill in a few other details. Did we spend the entire evening at the Club Cabana?"

"I can't remember," she confessed. "I think we decided to try a couple of other places when you said the wheel was cooling off, but I'm afraid I was pretty fuzzy by then."

I shrugged, "The hell with it. It'll probably come back slowly."

She agreed, sipped more coffee. I thought of Kent, frothing at the mouth when I failed to show up. My pleasure changed to uneasiness. He was quite capable of tearing down the Club Cabana brick by brick if he thought anything had happened to me there.

I said wistfully, "Doggone, the first time I really bust my harness in five years, I pull a mental blank. It's never happened to me before."

I put down the empty cup and scrambled to my feet. She left the rest of her coffee. I reached out my hand to help her up. She took the hand, and as she rose put her arms around my neck, kissed me full on the mouth, and stepped out of reach.

I was too surprised to move. Her voice was merry again, as I remembered it from the night before. "Please stay here, Chet. I'll be ready in a few minutes."

Feeling considerably let down, I piled the dishes into the sink. Something bothered me, but to save my life I couldn't put my finger on it. Of this I was sure: I had been kissed to shut my mouth, to prevent my asking further questions. It suddenly dawned on me that this situation was loaded with dynamite if it should ever come to the attention of the proper parties.

The problem was no nearer solution when the Gail reappeared, fully dressed. She said, "I'd like to go home, please. Do you mind taking me?"

I thought glumly, It doesn't make much difference what I do now. If this proves some sort of frameup, the details have long since been attended to. I retrieved my coat, hunted around for my hat. I had been wearing a brown one. A brown one of a lighter shade lay near my coat, not mine, though it fitted reasonably well. I put it on without comment.

We went out into the hall and took an automatic elevator to the street. I mentally noted the address as the Gail led me to a sporty little coupe parked halfway down the block. The neighborhood was a quiet residential one, convenient to the business district about fifteen minutes away by bus.

We climbed into the car, and the Gail started the motor. I didn't feel conversationally inclined, and she made no effort to break into my silence. I thought desperately, I've got to remember what happened. The best I could dig up was a chaotic impression of people milling about. By now, my only worry was lest I had involved Kent in my stupid escapade.

The car turned a corner, stopped before a big house. I reached forward to open the door. Before I could get a hand on it, it was yanked wide from outside. Two cops stood on the sidewalk. Other cops swarmed on the far side. A prowl car, siren wailing, came tearing down the block. I had only a second in which to look at the Gail. Her eyes were wide and blank. A hand reached inside, closed on my arm.

"Come on, buddy," the cop said; "make it snappy."

"Let go of me, you baboon," I snarled, trying to shake myself free. "I'm a reporter."

I was out on the sidewalk. Another cop anchored my left arm. He said soothingly, "Take it easy. Nobody's gonna hurt you. We just wanna ask you a few questions."

I struggled to release myself. "Questions about what?"
"Murder," said the cop. "Just a little case of murder."

---

# CHAPTER 3

---

I SAID to the cop at the door, "Who's been knocked off, chum?"
He gave me a strange look. "Jeffrey Dillon, didn't you know?
I thought you was a reporter."

I said, "Yeah, but I don't get around as much as I used to. Besides, the Free Press is a family newspaper."

We were in a small room just off the foyer. Through the closed door I heard a babel of voices and the heavy tramp of many feet. Outside, another siren wailed notice of reinforcements arriving.

I lit a cigarette, picked me a comfortable chair, tilted my hat over my eyes. Jeffrey Dillon murdered! I wondered whether the news came as a surprise to his daughter. She didn't fit the part, but I had seen more than one cold-blooded gal killer who looked as though she'd faint at the sight of a cut finger.

A voice said, "Well, I'll be double damned."

I glanced up, and there, big as life and twice as unpleasant, was beefy, red-faced Lieutenant Dennis Shanahan of the Homicide Squad.

I pushed my hat back. "Hiya, Knife."

He slammed his fists against his flanks and started bellowing at the astonished cops. "I told you to keep reporters out. And especially this bastard." He glared at me with sudden suspicion. "I thought you and your screwball boss was in Seattle."

One of the cops found his voice. "I'm trying to tell you, Lieutenant," he said plaintively, "this is the guy come with Miss Dillon. He said he was a reporter, but we figured it for a stall."

Knife said slowly, "He come with Miss Dillon, eh?" He rubbed a huge hand over his bristling chin. "Well, that's different, of course." He dropped his paw on my shoulder. "I'm certainly glad to see you, Chet, my boy."

"Knife," I said, "a little birdie tells me you're up to no good."

He pulled up a chair but made no motion to send the cops out. He said, very casually, "There's a couple of small matters I'd like to check up with you."

"You know I'm always glad to help along the cause of justice, Knife." He bridled, but let it pass. "Suppose you start by telling me where you and Miss Dillin've been. Her family was awful worried when she didn't show up last night."

"Was her pop worried, too?" I inquired.

He nodded solemnly. "You bet he was. That's why we're here." His manner became confidential. "He was scared she might of got herself kidnapped."

The cop at the door was making noises, unsuccessfully trying to attract Knife's attention. I yawned, flipped my hat forward again. I said, "You can't pull those old back room tricks on me, Knife. I know Dillon was murdered. You're trying to trap me. I'm entitled to a lawyer before I answer any questions."

He sprang to his feet, yanked me out of the chair. "How do you know he was murdered?" he barked. "There ain't been time to print it in the papers yet. Did Gail Dillon tell you?"

The cop said in a dead voice, "I guess we told him. We thought maybe he'd say something."

Knife flung me back into the chair. I sprawled out, pretending complete collapse.

A purple flush started just above Knife's collar and mounted to his hair. He shook his head in helpless wonder. He was beyond anger. The cop mumbled, "Give us ten minutes with him, Lieutenant. He'll talk."

Knife recovered speech. "Shut up," he roared. He stood over me with doubled fists. "Get up, you yellow-belly."

Whatever his intentions, Knife had no opportunity to put them into effect. There was a commotion outside the door and Kent burst in, with two frantic plainclothes dicks trying to head him off and yet not touch him.

Kent brushed aside the dicks and walked directly over to Knife. He said simply, "I have twenty million dollars. If you have injured this man, I am willing to spend every dollar of it to insure the punishment your bestiality merits."

Knife's eyes popped. His voice cracked. "I didn't even touch him."

Kent came over and sniffed the air above me. I sat up. "I am not drunk," I said indignantly. "He knocked me down. I'm trying to get my wind back."

More cops and dicks pushed into the tiny room. Kent snorted. He said, "What is the meaning of this performance? Of what are you accused and why are you simulating injury?"

I answered the last question first. "I'm not simulating. He really knocked me down. If I hadn't had enough sense to stay down, you'd be spending those twenty millions right now." I ignored Knife's ferocious gestures. "You must have gotten a flash about Dillon being murdered. Knife thinks I know all about it because I arrived a little while ago with Dillon's daughter."

Kent said judiciously, "I see. Most unfortunate." I knew better. A murder with one of his reporters on the inside is the cherished dream of every publisher in the world, and Kent was no exception. "I think, Lieutenant," he said with an air of deference, "we might better conduct our discussion under more favorable conditions, eh?" He raised his eyebrows at the audience of gaping cops.

A little oil went a long way with Knife. He swelled up, started issuing orders, had the room cleared. He sat down heavily and motioned Kent to a chair. He said with suddenly reawakened suspicion, "Who told you Phelps was here?"

Kent said, "A reporter from the Free Press glimpsed him and phoned me. The circumstances seemed peculiar enough to warrant my personal investigation."

Knife snarled, "Them damn reporters are like buzzards, crawling all over the joint and getting in the way. What's this feller's name who seen him?"

"Cafferty. You'll find him outside. Don't you think we should let Chet tell his story?"

Knife agreed reluctantly, "All right, but he better make it good." He turned to me. "Let's have it."

"Well," I began, "Mr. Kent and I had dinner last night at the restaurant next to the Club Cabana. Afterwards he returned to the office, and I thought I'd kill some time in the club. You can check that part easily enough with Commissioner Osmond and District Attorney Hendrickson, who were there, too."

Knife flushed. "I'll take your word for it."

I grinned and went on to describe my chance meeting with the Gail and the brawl at the roulette table, all of which I placed around eleven o'clock. About my conversation with Firelli and the proposition offered by Jerry Candle and Roy Meade I thought it wiser to say nothing.

"I remember playing a while longer and having a few drinks with Miss Dillon. The next thing I knew was when I woke up an hour or so ago in a strange apartment on Montgomery Street."

Knife said, "Wait a minute. You mean you passed out at the Cabana and came to in a strange apartment with a dame you never seen up to last night, huh?"

"I have no recollection of passing out or even being sick. I'm sure I was drugged. One moment I was at the bar having a drink, and the next it was morning. There's absolutely nothing in between."

Knife fumbled in his pocket, drew out an evil-looking cigar, bit off the end. He let Kent produce a lighter and hold it while he puffed. From Kent's expression you'd never have guessed he had fired good men for coming into his office smelling of cigar smoke.

Knife grunted through the cigar, "We haven't fixed the exact time yet, but Dillon was killed during the night. Your man here"— he pointed his stogie at me—"shoots us a line about waking up with the guy's daughter in some empty apartment. It don't sound right. I got to hold him."

"Suit yourself," said Kent, suddenly indifferent. He stood up, giving Knife a glance of mild pity. "I infer you are not interested in the suggestion I had intended to offer." He started for the door.

"Hey, wait a minute," Knife shouted.

Kent turned part way. "I do not for a moment believe Phelps is involved in this business. However, I appreciate the necessity for an active effort to clear his name and, by extension, that of the Free Press. This we cannot accomplish without also solving the murder in which he stands implicated."

"We'll solve the murder," Knife said doggedly.

"I'm sure you will," Kent echoed. "Nevertheless, to protect itself, the Free Press will conduct its own investigation, if need be with professional aid. You may rest assured expense will not deter us."

Knife said dramatically, "Words, words! What's your proposition?"

"I am coming to it. Your cooperation would render drastic steps unnecessary. Release Phelps in my custody. I unconditionally guarantee to produce him upon request. Under those conditions all the facilities of the Free Press will be placed at your disposal. And when you have apprehended the culprit, as I am certain you will, the Free Press will place proper emphasis on your success."

While Knife revolved this in his mind, I followed up swiftly. "You know, Mr. Kent is a man of his word. Play your cards smart and you'll come out of this a captain or better."

Kent nodded sagely. Knife licked his lips. He clamped the cigar back in his face with sudden decision, and offered his hand. "It's a deal!"

Kent, smiling, clasped the proferred hand warmly. "You will not regret it, sir. And now"—he glanced delicately at his wrist watch

—"we have no time to lose if we intend to question the members of the family." He patted Knife's back. "How right of you to insist on immediate action. Lead the way, Lieutenant."

---

# CHAPTER 4

---

KNIFE said, "Seeing as we're pulling together, Mr. Kent, I don't mind admitting this is the damndest killing ever." He led the way through a corridor toward a part of the house where all the activity seemed concentrated. "We're holding the family upstairs. The body was discovered in the library by this Swede maid about seven a.m."

From Knife's remarks I was prepared for violence, but nothing like the spectacle that had prompted the Swedish maid's fits. The body was there—a hideous thing bearing little resemblance to a man—sprawled on its back on the floor before a big desk, with two police photographers buzzing around it, like busy flies. However, it wasn't the corpse or the bloodstained poker beside it that created horror, but the grinning false faces—at first glance it seemed like hundreds of them—staring from the walls, the floor, smeared on the seat of every one of the cream leather chairs. The faces were painted with gaping round mouths in a hideous caricature of laughter.

Kent let his breath out, all in one piece as though he had been kicked in the stomach. I followed his gaze to the floor and saw now separately what had only been part of a total dizzy first impression —another false face identical with those about the room painted over the pulp that had been the corpse's own face.

Even without the false faces or body, the room rated attention. Had a giant hand shaken it, the place could not have been more thoroughly wrecked. Furniture was up-ended and smashed, hundreds of books were pulled down from shelves lining all four walls, pictures torn from their supports.

Knife said behind me, "Ain't it the damnedest damn thing you ever seen?"

I agreed without taking my eyes from the scene. As nearly as I could judge, the false faces had been drawn with some kind of black grease. They followed a crude general pattern, a circle to indicate the head, two spots for the eyes, a single long slash for the nose. An inner circle formed the laughing mouth, a thick smear above it a moustache. A blob below the mouth appeared intended for a beard. Neither ears nor hair had been drawn in.

A pair of plainclothes dicks squatting on their haunches patiently sorted out the garbage underfoot, putting each examined scrap of paper in one pile, bits of glass and assorted junk in another. They didn't seem to mind our presence. The police photographers finished with their pictures and dropped a sheet carelessly over the body.

Kent said, "A horrible crime, unbelievable." He sounded as though he were offering congratulations. He lived under the impression that all major catastrophes were deliberately designed to help him sell papers.

Knife took him literally. He said, "Yeah, ain't it awful? Honest, I'm disgusted." He addressed the photographers. "Are you through?"

"Yeah, just finished. The wagon's on the way up."

"About time. Let's get it the hell out of here. It's cluttering up the joint."

I asked, remembering the battered features, "Who made the identification?"

"His wife. No doubt about it. Since the Murphy stink, all lawyers practicing in the criminal courts got to register their fingerprints."

Kent asked, "Has the specific cause of death been determined yet?"

Knife said, no, they were certain only that Dillon had already been dead when two bullets were pumped into his body at close range, since there had been no bleeding from the wound. The Medical Examiner, now administering to the hysterical Swedish maid, had thrown up his hands at sight of the corpse. Obviously, death had occurred many hours before, but the delay in finding the body made setting the time of murder a difficult laboratory matter. Similarly, the excessive violence had obscured the cause of death, though Simpson had hazarded strangulation.

"Hell," Knife exclaimed, "I'll bet you a hat right now we'll probably find the chump was poisoned when we open him up." He lowered his voice and spoke to Kent. "I got a kind of theory."

"Really?" Kent lifted his eyebrows.

"Well, it ain't such a hot theory," Knife conceded, "but you got to start some place. Let's say Phelps and this blonde just happened to be off on a binge and forget about them. Who have you got left?

Why, the old lady, of course."

Kent said, "I fancy you mean the widowed Mrs. Dillon?"

"Sure. Everybody knows old Dillon was playing around with this chicken—what's her name?"

"Antoine St. Arles," I supplied.

Knife said, "Yeah, that one. So all right, the old battleaxe don't go for it, see?" He emphasized his words with a stabbing forefinger. "She ships the family out, gets rid of the servants—"

Kent said, "One moment, Lieutenant. Am I to understand the house was deserted for a good part of the evening?"

"Sure, didn't I tell you? Anyway, she gets rid of everybody, comes back in, slips the old guy a mickey and then busts up the joint to make it look like a struggle."

"Does she have an alibi?" Kent wanted to know.

"Well, yeah," Knife admitted, "but we'll work on it now. She claims she et dinner with some crowd she used to go to school with and they caught a late pitcher show at the Bijou. Them kind of alibis ain't worth the powder to blow them to hell."

Two white-coated stretcher bearers from the city morgue arrived. We retraced our steps along the corridor, to the front stairs. I said to Knife as we marched single file, "By the way, what picture was missing from the frame between the windows?"

Knife said unguardedly, "Some kind of banquet photo; we're tracking it down now." He assumed a belatedly wary expression, clamped his lips shut. Kent appeared perplexed. It had escaped his attention. I had noticed the frame on the far wall between two windows hanging from one corner of its support, its smashed glass on the floor. At first I assumed the picture had been torn from its backing during the struggle; then I saw the razor-fine line around the molding. Whatever picture the frame had held had been deliberately cut out and removed. My spirits rose an inch or two when I discerned a slight gleam of approval in Kent's cold eyes.

# CHAPTER 5

A STOLID cop admitted us to the sitting room where the Dillons were gathered. It was a big room, long and high, with an elaborate fireplace at one end. Veronica Dillon and a solid, lawyerish-looking person occupied a sofa arrangement flank-

ing it. Over by the windows, a good fifteen feet away, a couple shared
a window bench. The Gail slumped in a big chair near a grand piano
which seemed the geographically farthest point from either of the
groups. Her nose and eyes were red, probably from crying. Her
hands, tight in her lap, clasped a twisted lace handkerchief. At a
small desk near the door, a polite stenographer in uniform fussed
over some notes.

The Gail's eyes lifted as I closed the door behind us. She appeared
momentarily surprised, as though she had expected to find me in
handcuffs, but she quickly turned her head, plucking at the handkerchief. The couple at the window talked together in undertones,
not bothering to stop at our entrance. Only Mrs. Dillon was visibly
affected. Seeing Knife, she swelled up, and poured the vials of her
wrath over his unprotected head.

Knife said, "Lady, we don't like this no better than you do. But
we gotta follow a routine." Recalling Kent's unexplained presence,
he introduced him in cautious syllables, ignoring me completely,
for which I was duly grateful. It developed that the couple at the
window were Raymond Dillon and his fiancée, Miss Laura Todd. He
was a nice-looking boy of twenty-some-odd, with dark, wavy hair
and a pleasant smile. Laura Todd I catalogued as just another Junior
League number.

Morgan said in his best courtroom manner, "Surely, Lieutenant,
there can be no further point in subjecting Mrs. Dillon to this ordeal.
She should be under a doctor's care instead of exposed to the strain
of continuous questioning."

Mama Veronica was a stylish stout of around forty with blue,
misty-looking eyes peering out from crinkles of fat, and hair whose
bright metallic blondeness was a shade too perfect. At Morgan's
words she wilted visibly, in the traditional posture of the bereaved
widow.

The harassed Knife said, "We'd get through faster if you people
cooperated more. The way you act anybody'd think I done the croak
—I mean killing. Now you, Mrs. Dillon—"

He launched into a painstaking playback of her already declared
alibi, no doubt for Kent's benefit, made her describe in the fullest
detail her movements from the time she had left the house, about
six o'clock, until her return after one.

Boiled down to its essentials, her story was the one Knife had
sketched in synopsis—dinner with Agnes Shelby, an old schoolmate,
a late movie at the Bijou where "Heart's A-twine" was the current
feature, a jawing session with Agnes who, it developed, had mort-

gage worries, and so home to bed. She had noticed nothing wrong and no light in the library. She and Jeffrey had separate bedrooms.

The Gail moved behind Knife on silent feet, went around the piano, and joined me on the bench.

She whispered urgently, "I must see you—afterwards."

I ducked my head to show I had heard her. She continued, "Phone me this afternoon, as soon as you can—I must tell you—"

Knife twisted around. He said, "You two got to stay apart; otherwise you'll have to leave, Phelps."

The Gail threw him a venomous look, and returned to her chair.

Knife was about finished with Veronica. He looked exhausted. He turned to Raymond. "Now then, there are a couple of things I want you to clear up for me. Suppose you explain a little better how you come to pick last night to call on the St. Arles dame."

Raymond fixed his gaze on the floor. "It was an unfortunate coincidence. Shortly before ten o'clock I spoke with my father over the phone. He sounded unhappy and worried. It seemed—well, heartless for all of us to go about our own affairs and leave him sitting alone brooding over his troubles."

"How did you know he was alone?"

"He said so, I believe. Oh yes, Laura wanted to ask Mother something. Father then mentioned he was alone in the house and expected to leave shortly."

"All right, what happened next?"

"I talked the matter over with my fiancée and her mother. I felt certain Miss St. Arles was the cause of my father's anxiety. I knew he had been trying to avoid her of late." He paused uncertainly.

"Go on," Knife encouraged him.

Raymond flushed. "Neither Laura nor her mother approved, but I was determined to have it out with Miss St. Arles. I left at once and arrived at her apartment about ten o'clock." He smiled ruefully. "Laura was right about the uselessness of my errand. Miss St. Arles insisted her dealings with my father were wholly of a business nature—none of my business, in other words. I soon realized I was making a fool of myself and left. Laura and I had a late date at the Gingley-Plaza. I picked her up, but before we started out I phoned my father again."

"When was this?"

"It must have been close to eleven."

"What did he say?"

Raymond shrugged. "He was furious. He told me to keep my nose out of his affairs and lots more in the same vein. Finally he slammed the receiver on me."

Morgan said, "I can offer corroborative evidence. I had reason to phone Jeffrey just about that time. The wire was busy for some little while—it was several minutes before I managed to reach him."

Knife did not ask the purpose of Morgan's late call but resumed his questioning of Raymond, who now related how he and Laura Todd had driven in her car to the Gingley-Plaza, where they arrived about half past eleven. Laura added that she might still have the parking stub stamped with the time of their arrival.

Further questioning established a minimum of twenty minutes' driving time from Todd's home to the Dillon manse and fifteen minutes more from the Dillons' to the Gingley-Plaza Hotel. I didn't follow these technical details closely, but they seemed to prove that even with Laura's connivance Raymond could not have left his fiancée's home after eleven, killed his father, painted the false faces and still put in an appearance at the Gingley-Plaza Hotel all within half an hour.

The Gail suddenly said, "I spoke to my father about the same time Raymond and Mr. Morgan mentioned."

Knife asked sourly, "You didn't by any chance call him, too, did you, Mrs. Dillon?"

Veronica retorted tartly that she had not.

A plainclothes dick came in and beckoned to Knife. He got up, and the two stood in the doorway, where they held a whispered consultation. After a while Knife came back and announced dramatically, "We got some news from Mr. Dillon's bank that changes the whole picture. His account shows withdrawals of over two hundred thousand dollars in the last year, all cash. It looks like we run up against a blackmail angle."

I watched Veronica, on whom it was dawning that she had been cheated of being a rich widow. She heaved herself erect. She was fit to be tied. She said to no one in particular, "I told you she would get his money, every cent of it. That whore." Her face contorted. She loosed a string of foul words.

Raymond sat paralyzed. Laura Todd looked as though she were about to faint. The Gail seized her mother's arms and shook her.

"How dare you say such things?" she cried. Veronica backed away, closed her mouth. There was a dangerous light in the Gail's narrowed eyes. She said, with deadly calm, "If Father was mixed up with her, you drove him to it. You hated and despised him. He wasn't blackmailed. He used his money to buy some of the happiness he never received at home."

In two long strides Raymond was at her side. He struck her mouth a blow that echoed through the room. I reached him barely in time to knock down the arm pulled back to hit her again.

I said, "This is exactly what we needed." I shoved him, unresisting, back toward his girl friend.

The Gail slowly returned to her chair. She said in a low voice, "I deserved it. I was beastly."

Veronica sighed. "You children will be the death of me yet."

It had all happened too fast for Knife. He roared furiously, "I think you're all slaphappy. But I'll get to the bottom of this mess if it takes a week."

A timid knock sounded at the door. Knife, in the act of lighting a fresh cigar, shouted, "Come in." Hendrickson, hat in hand, entered, smiling apologetically.

Knife practically fell over himself in his eagerness to welcome aid. "Folks," he boomed, "I want you to meet the D.A. himself."

Hendrickson winced. He said, "Ah, thank you, Lieutenant." He nodded warmly as each person was introduced, said, "Mr. Morgan and I are old courtroom opponents."

Knife said, "Have a cigar, Mr. Hendrickson."

Hendrickson paled. He said faintly, "Thank you, no." He threw a troubled glance in the direction of Kent, piped, "If you will all excuse me, I should like a few words alone with Lieutenant Shanahan," and drew Knife outside.

The Gail turned and looked at me. I nodded briefly. Nobody spoke.

# CHAPTER 6

H ENDRICKSON said thoughtfully, "I see. I see." When he spoke, the tip of his nose quivered. He had finished leading Veronica through another exhausting account of her activities on the previous evening. I felt as though I had been to the Bijou with her.

Hendrickson said, "I have no wish to detain you further, Mrs. Dillon." His voice dripped sympathy. "You may retire to your room and rest if you like."

Laura Todd went over to Veronica's side and helped her up. Hendrickson nodded approval as she guided Veronica to the door. "I'll be back in a few minutes," Laura promised.

Hendrickson glanced at his notes. "Mr. Dillon, you spoke of your father's troubled mental state prior to his death. Would you mind repeating it for my benefit?"

Raymond looked at him with undisguised contempt. He said, "My impression was that he worried chiefly over his relationship with Miss St. Arles." He grimaced. "Like a fool, I thought I could do something about it."

Hendrickson said brightly, "I see."

The Gail raised her head. "I can tell you what you want to know. Father was in constant fear of his life. Ever since things started breaking badly for him."

"Like the traction fix?" I inserted.

"The traction thing was merely the final blow. He was being deliberately undermined. His friends and associates were turning against him."

Morgan puffed out his cheeks and began spluttering. "Really, I must protest, Mr. District Attorney. As Jeffrey's closest associate, I feel that Miss Dillon's suspicions are obviously directed against me."

Hendrickson said quietly, "I'm sure Miss Dillon intends no actual accusation." He encouraged the Gail with a reassuring smile. "Won't you try to be more specific?"

She took a convulsive breath as Morgan turned injured eyes on her. "I can't say exactly. I'm not a lawyer, but in cases Father should have won easily, his clients went to jail or jumped their bail, witnesses turned against him on the stand. Things like that, and others he didn't mention but implied."

Hendrickson and Morgan exchanged amused glances. The Gail said heatedly, "I know what I'm talking about. He once told me he was being turned into a scapegoat."

Morgan lifted his voice. "If you will permit be, I can throw some light on this matter. Until recently, when Jeffrey went into voluntary semi-retirement, I shared his confidence to a greater degree than most others."

Hendrickson pursed his lips, nodded gravely. "By all means."

"The fact is, Jeffrey Dillon suffered from a delusion. In my considered opinion, he was in a state of mental collapse."

The Gail shouted, "You're a liar." She appealed to Kent. "Please don't let them say such things about my father."

"Mr. Hendrickson is not likely to believe that a man was murdered by a delusion," Kent said with a faint smile.

Hendrickson slapped the arm of his chair. "This is intolerable, Mr. Kent. If you interfere, I shall be compelled to ask you to leave. You may continue, Mr. Morgan."

Morgan looked unhappy. "Jeffrey felt himself responsible for the heavy losses incurred by his clients as a result of the Free Press attack on the traction unification project. He became hypersensitive and finally fell into the delusion that everybody was in a conspiracy against him."

"Ah, yes. A persecution complex," Hendrickson said sagely.

"Precisely. Naturally, his efforts at the bar faltered, and then he lost cases he should have won easily."

"When was the last time you were in communication with Mr. Dillon?"

"Last night, about eleven o'clock." Morgan hesitated. "I spoke with him earlier in the evening, and we arranged an appointment for eleven-thirty at my apartment. I phoned at eleven to make certain he intended to come."

"Was the nature of the appointment such as to have any bearing on his death?"

Morgan hesitated again. He said finally, "In my opinion, no. Needless to say, he failed to keep the appointment."

Hendrickson said, "And you know of no person with reason to kill him?"

Morgan said positively, "No, I do not."

"And you, Miss Dillon—or Mr. Dillon?" He looked from one to the other. "Can either of you suggest any possible motive for your father's death?"

Raymond shook his head, looked dazed. The Gail said in a flat voice, "You suspect me. You haven't believed anything I've told you."

Hendrickson raised one eyebrow. "I am not aware of having accused you, Miss Dillon. But since you raise the question, I must confess your hostility does nothing to strengthen your position." He consulted his notes. "Are you still unable to account for your whereabouts during the greater part of last night?"

She bit her lip, looking at me in silent appeal. I said, "We were drugged. Why not ask your friend, Firelli, for the details?"

Hendrickson put down his notes, and gave me his full attention. He said with ominous calm, "I am not ready for you yet, Phelps." He turned back to the Gail, suggested more kindly, "Perhaps if you tell us a little of how you spent the earlier part of the evening, your mind will be refreshed concerning later events."

"Father and I were the only ones in the house," she began. "We had dinner together at seven-thirty. Afterwards he said he had some work to finish in the library. I went up to my room."

"At what time did you leave?"

"A little after half past nine. I had an appointment at the Club Cabana. When I had finished dressing, I came downstairs and started to enter the library to say good night, but paused when I heard Father talking over the phone."

"With whom was he talking?" Hendrickson interjected.

She gazed directly at Morgan. "I don't know."

"Did you ascertain the nature of the conversation?"

After a moment's hesitation, she shook her head. "I decided to leave without disturbing him. Since it was a little early for my date, I drove into the country for a while. I got to the Club Cabana about a quarter to eleven and tried to phone my father. The line was busy for almost fifteen minutes. I finally reached him and asked whether he was all right. He said I was a ninny and told me to stop worrying."

Laura Todd entered, walked across the room to Raymond, and sat down beside him. He looked at her inquiringly, and she nodded and took his hand.

Hendrickson fussed with his notes. He said casually, "Was Mr. Phelps waiting for you at the Club?"

The Gail said promptly, "Yes, at the roulette table."

If I hadn't been sitting, I would have fainted. Knife's eyes bugged out. Even Kent looked faintly surprised. The Gail wore an air of complete innocence.

Hendrickson was enjoying his moment of triumph. He said, "There seems to be a slight discrepancy between your statement and the account Phelps gave Lieutenant Shanahan. I think, Miss Dillon, you had better tell us some more about this appointment."

The Gail studied his face as though for a clue. She said, puzzled, "I don't understand. Chet and I became acquainted about a year ago. Yesterday afternoon he phoned and suggested we meet at the Club Cabana about ten-thirty." Guilty realization showed in her manner as she looked from me to Hendrickson. "Is anything wrong?"

I thought fast. I said nonchalantly, "Well, if she doesn't mind, I guess it's all right with me, too. Things being as they were last year, we decided to keep our friendship quiet. What with the libel action and all, I thought it best to resume on the same basis." I sat back with a virtuous smirk.

"You should rehearse your stories better," Hendrickson observed sarcastically. "What of this apartment where you claim to have found yourselves this morning?"

She said quickly, "It's my apartment. I rented it several months ago under the name of Clarice Dill."

Raymond gaped as though he were seeing his sister for the first time. Laura studiously looked out the window. Hendrickson blushed, and cleared his throat nervously. He said, "I am forced to ask this final question. Had you and Phelps planned to go to your apartment last night?"

She said faintly, "No. I have no recollection of arriving there."

"And you, Phelps?"

"I'll stick to my story. We were drugged."

Hendrickson made an exasperated noise. He said, "Perhaps, then, you might also tell me why you were drugged. And while you are explaining, I should like to know your relationship with two such notorious gangsters as Jerry Candle and Roy Meade."

I pretended to concentrate. "Oh, those two." I laughed. "We got to chinning while I waited for Miss Dillon and had a drink together. If you knew they were gangsters, why didn't you have them picked up last night?"

Hendrickson said stiffly, "If you don't mind, I'll ask the questions. Fortunately for you, I agree with Lieutenant Shanahan in thinking that blackmail is at the root of this murder." He turned to Kent. "Was all the information available on the traction contracts used at the time?"

Kent said with open contempt, "I publish the news. I do not hoard it."

Hendrickson rose. He said, "You are all at liberty to go about your business. However, I ask you not to leave the city without my specific permission until further notice."

If there was a murderer in the room, his facial expression did not betray him.

# CHAPTER 7

 SMALL mob of reporters and cameramen milled around Hendrickson as we left the room.

I grunted and dived back into the push to rescue Kent

from the badgerings of half a dozen rival sheet legmen. Outside, I said, "Where do we go from here?"

"I should'like to drop in at the Albermarle Apartments," Kent informed me.

I said with admiration, "The Albermarle—well, well."

The Albermarle Apartments, a high-class pile overlooking River Drive, was the address of two thirds of the kept women in town. Nine stories high, it had a swell view of the river and a saluting doorman in mauve livery. Antoine St. Arles lived there in a three room layout on the fourth floor.

Kent hailed a cab. He settled himself, let me give the driver our destination and prepared to spend a happy fifteen minutes touching up his rosy nails.

Our cab turned into River Drive. I said, "I gather, O Noble Intelligence, that we are supposed to interview La Antoine. How do you propose to go about it?"

"I am a publisher, not a reporter," Kent said acidly. "However, I believe the accepted practise is to inform the person at the switchboard that a representative of the Free Press requests a few minutes of Miss St. Arle's time."

We drew up before the Albermarle. Through the side window I saw the crowd camping in the lobby leap up like a pack on a fresh scent. The saluting doorman was nowhere in sight. I leaned forward and yelled to our driver, "Start rolling, fast."

Kent indignantly tapped on the window. "Pull around the corner," he ordered.

"Listen, boss," I pleaded, "you're in this deep enough. Don't be silly. You haven't a chance against that mob of newshawks."

"I had no intention of going in," he said placidly. "I'll wait here."

"That's the executive technique, isn't it? You haven't a cockeyed notion in the world how to crash the joint, but figure if you act like it's a cinch, I'll have to produce."

"Cafferty could do it."

"Don't needle me," I retorted. "I'm going. If I'm not back in an hour, look for me in the clink. Bring plenty of bail money." I climbed out stiffly.

I turned the corner, went over to the park side of the drive and sauntered toward the Albermarle. I kept walking, turned the next corner and strolled along, still on the opposite side of the street, until I located my goal—the Albermarle's service entrance. I also found the doorman and an overalled porter on guard.

I kept walking clear across to Garfield Road, a matter of half a mile, before I located a hardware store. Here I bought two hundred feet of white, insulated wire, an ordinary tin tool box and four dollars worth of assorted junk—hammers, screw drivers, pliers, washers and the like. I slung the wire over my shoulder and hiked back across town.

The doorman still barred the service entrance of the Albermarle. I asked amiably, "What'sa trouble?"

He refused to unbend. "Where you going, feller?"

I took a notebook from my hip pocket, wet my forefinger, and flipped the pages. "Got a line complaint from Three-B."

The porter volunteered, "That's Jeannette Ackley in Three-B."

The doorman considered, "Okay, Jimmy here will take you up, but I don't know will she let you in. She sleeps mornings."

"Never mind, I'll find my way."

"Sorry, I gotta send Jimmy along. There's a dame in Four-G every reporter in town is trying to reach, and we gotta be careful nobody crashes."

We rode the service elevator to the third floor, where we marched along the corridor to a door labelled Three-B. Jimmy pushed the bell button with a grimy finger, and whispered, "Boy, is this a dish."

An irritated voice from within screamed, "Cut out the damn ringing. I'm coming." The peephole opened, and hostile eyes stared out.

"Telephone Company," Jimmy whined. I elbowed him aside and raised my hat. "Checking on the line, Miss Ackley."

The eyes inspected me, withdrew. Jimmy shrugged, but a moment later the door opened.

"You can come in," she ordered. As Jimmy tried to follow, she pushed him back. "Who are you, Filthy," she demanded, "the Coat Holder?" She slammed the door on him. "The phone is over there on the table."

I crossed the room without looking at her, set the tool box and wire on the floor. I took the phone off its cradle, balanced it, listened thoughtfully to the dial tone. Behind me I heard the clink of bottle against glass and decided she was pouring herself an eye opener. I turned and found her watching me critically from the depths of a big chair.

"Have a spot?"

I said, "No ma'am," and grinned. She was a honey, small-boned and dark and sleek as a kitten. She wore a thin silk robe that clung in all the right places.

I moved the table out of the way, and fumbled along the wall until I found the bell box.

"Where's your phone set?"

I got up from the floor, gulped, and stammered, "I don't need a phone set for this kind of job, lady." I bent down, selected a screwdriver, and subjected it to a critical inspection.

She said, "Hey, wait a minute. Are you sure you can put it together again? I need the phone."

"Lady," I proclaimed, "I been doing this man and boy for twelve years. You hurt me."

She laughed, "I'll bet I do," and smoothed the robe over her hips. I flung the screwdriver back in the box. She poured two drinks, coaxing, "Come on, big boy, one jolt won't do you any harm. You look like you need it."

I took the drink. She was right. I needed it.

She said, "What's your name?"

"Davis—Richard Harding Davis. The boys call me Dick."

"That's a nice name, Dick. Come here and sit down. You're no telephone repairman. What's the gag?"

I thought, What the hell, and sat down by her. "I wanted to meet you, and this was the only way of doing it," I said contritely.

She gurgled, "Oh boy, just like the movies," and grabbed me in a headlock.

When she came up for air, I said, "The porter was suspicious, Jeannette. The place is overrun by reporters on account of some dame upstairs whose boy friend got knocked off."

That had the desired effect. She jumped up, saying, "Damn the luck. You better leave."

I closed the tool box, trying to act broken-hearted. She went out into the corridor and stood by the hall door. As I started to open it, she put her hand on my arm and swayed toward me. I kissed her hard, and mumbled, "Where can we meet?"

"The Circus Bar, four o'clock," she breathed.

I finally put the door between us and mopped my brow. Life was certainly in high gear at the Albermarle. I catfooted it up one flight to the fourth floor, hoping that La Antoine had not decided to skip while I was occupied with Lady Casanova. La Antoine's apartment, Four-G, faced the elevator on the river side. I cached the wire and tools and rang her bell. The peephole opened immediately.

I took off my hat and said rapidly, "John Perry from Mr. Morgan's office. I have a message for you."

The door opened a crack and I slid in. She said brusquely, "What's your message?"

Five years ago, when Dillon met her, she must have been been a sultry beauty. Now she was edging toward plumpness and little puffs under the eyes.

There was nothing to be gained by stalling. "There is no message, Miss St. Arles," I admitted. "I'm Chet Phelps from the Free Press."

She didn't throw any fits. She asked, "How did you get in?" She started to open the door.

"I know a back way. Look, before you pitch me out, give me a chance to explain. The Free Press has a proposition for you. We tried to phone, but couldn't reach you."

"What kind of a proposition?"

"Your life story. Why hand out free interviews to those vultures downstairs? We'll pay you handsomely for exclusive rights to your life story."

She came directly to the point. "How much?"

"You'll have to make arrangements with Mr. Kent. He's not downtown now, but you can reach him this afternoon."

"Maybe I will," she said thoughtfully. "I have to look out for myself." She shot me a veiled glance. "You don't think I had any part in it, do you?"

"Absolutely not," I lied. "You're in the clear."

"You bet I'm in the clear." There was belligerence in her voice. "I can prove where I was every minute. I spent the evening with Tom Morgan."

"After Raymond Dillon came to see you?" I prompted.

"Yes." She looked sullen. "Quit pumping me."

"You're supposed to be Dillon's girl," I ventured. "How come you're so chummy with Morgan?"

She shrugged. "Dillon hasn't been around in six months."

I said, "You say you can prove where you were every minute of last night. What time did you leave here?"

"I don't have to tell you—but I will. I got home around eight and didn't leave until ten-thirty."

"Nobody cares about the time before eleven. Dillon was still alive then, because three people talked with him. How's your alibi for after eleven?"

"All right, wise guy. My alibi for after eleven is just as good. I went to Tom's apartment at ten-thirty and stayed there until almost one o'clock. Then I took a cab from right in front of his door and came straight back here."

"Was Morgan at his place when you arrived?"

"You ask too goddamn many questions."

"All right, skip it."

"No, I won't. Sure he was there. He was waiting for Dillon. I was with him when he talked to Dillon at eleven." She peered at me cunningly. "What do you think of that?"

"It checks. Where does Raymond Dillon come in on all this?"

She chose her words carefully. "You want to know too much. Tell Kent I'll think over his proposition. If I like it, I'll call him. But I'll want the money on the line."

"That's okay with us."

She nodded, and closed the door. The colored boy on the service elevator took me down without comment. I dumped the prop tools and wire in an areaway and doubled back to where Kent was waiting.

He greeted me bitterly. "Where have you been? Or do you fancy I relish cooling my heels in a cab half the morning?"

"I used your system—sent up my name and requested a few minutes of her valuable time."

He smiled quizzically.

"You'll be glad to hear I practically contracted for her life story. Even if you don't want it, I shut her mouth long enough to put an edition on the street."

"Most unethical," he murmured. "However—"

"Don't 'however' me." I recited my conversation with her practically verbatim. "She seemed awful anxious to trot out her alibi for my inspection. Right up to where I asked whether Morgan was home when she got to his place. She sounded a little rattled then."

"Inconclusive." Kent looked discontented. "You are too prone to jump at conclusions."

I said, "For my money, Morgan is our man."

"Did he simply strangle his partner or also shoot him and crack his skull?"

I said with scorn, "Go on, hedge. I'm sorry I brought up the subject. What's my next move?"

"There is no next move for you."

"Don't worry about me. I can take care of myself."

"So I have noticed. Until we determine how the wind is blowing, I have decided your safest course is to do nothing the police might construe as provocative."

I muttered darkly, "I put you inside a big story and then get elbowed aside while you have all the fun."

Kent shrugged. "You have been clamoring for a rest. This is your opportunity. Make the most of it."

# CHAPTER 8

A HARNESS bull was leaning carelessly against the doorway of the Dillon manse. He straightened smartly but drooped again as he recognized me.

The Gail herself opened the door. When she saw me, she threw the door wide. "I'm so glad you could come, Chet."

"No trouble at all," I assured her.

She whispered in my ear, "Oh, darling, it's so good to see you again."

I unwound my arm. "Listen, Lucrezia Borgia, you and I have some chinning to do. The last time I asked you a question you kissed me quiet. Better start kissing right away."

She said, "Is that the only reason you came—to ask me questions?"

"You guessed it."

"Then you can leave."

I said with a show of indifference, "Suits me. If Kent learns I was anywhere near here, he'll skin me alive." I put my hand on the door knob.

"Wait." She covered my hand with her own. "Please, Chet, don't let's quarrel. I'll answer your questions."

She led the way to the sitting room. It looked bigger without all the people, and even a little friendlier. She moved to the sofa by the fireplace, sat down and motioned me to join her.

I said brusquely, "The first thing I want to know is why you told that cockeyed lie about having an appointment with me at the Cabana last night."

Tears sprang into her eyes. "I—I had no other choice. I knew the police would never believe I had gone there alone. I was sure you would stand by me."

I said grimly, "You must be nuts. What do you suppose will happen when Hendrickson checks your story?" I stopped. It was no use trying to show her the enormity of her error. I doubt if she heard me, she was crying so hard now.

I patted her head, and "there-there'd" for a while until she calmed down. I said, "It can't be helped now. That's your story and we're stuck with it, heaven help us."

She threw her arms around my neck. There was nothing restrained about her kiss. When she finally broke away, I said, "I hope I'll remember that when they throw the switch."

She laughed. I couldn't decide whether she was a good actress or just another addlewit.

I said, "Merely to satisfy my curiosity, why did you go to the Cabana last night? I mean, on the level, why?"

"I like to gamble. I do it every chance I get."

"Wouldn't it have been simpler to come right out and say so when you were questioned?"

"The family has never known." She looked smug, the idiot, as though she had put one over.

I tried a new tack. "You must have some idea about the murder. Whom do you suspect?"

"Everybody—nobody."

"I can see where you're going to be a big help. You were the last to see your father alive. You left here at nine-thirty. Granting you're telling the truth, there's better than an hour and a half unaccounted for, between nine-thirty and almost eleven when I met you. Where were you the rest of the time?"

She set her mouth in an obstinate line. "You heard what I told Mr. Hendrickson. I drove into the country."

I flung up my hands. "Don't tell me you actually think he swallowed that yarn? He's stalling until the autopsy. If he learns your father was killed less than an hour and a half after you left here, you'll hear plenty more about your hayride."

The tears were flowing freely again. I mechanically handed her a handkerchief. She dabbed at her eyes.

"Firelli was waiting for us downtown. Does that interest you?" She wept louder.

"He says we left the Cabana at twelve. You'd better start hoping Hendrickson finds the murder took place between eleven and twelve."

She said through the folds of the handkerchief, "Daddy couldn't have been killed before eleven. I talked with him. So did Raymond and Mr. Morgan."

"Voices can be faked."

She took the handkerchief away from her face. "I know my father's voice."

"If your father was alive at eleven, he may not have been killed until after midnight," I mused. "And we can't account for ourselves beyond that time. I've got to know what happened last night."

She said in a strained voice, "I have no recollection."

I said patiently, "Look, sister, this is no spot for modesty. Your whole family knows we spent the night together, and they'll feel the same about it whether we were drunk, sober or drugged. The question now is how we got there and what, if anything, happened in the interval."

She said with sudden decision, "I'll tell you everything I can. You were winning steadily at the table. You ordered drinks several times. When my luck turned, you suggested pooling our funds and splitting the winnings."

I nodded encouragement as she paused.

She took a deep breath. "On your plays we were about a thousand dollars ahead when the wheel turned against you. You went outside, and when you got back said you had had a drink at the bar. We played a while longer with a little better luck. You looked flushed, complained of the heat. It seemed time to cash in. This was about midnight. I wanted to leave at once, but you insisted we have a last drink together at the bar."

I said, "Most of this is news to me. I can recall as far as going out the first time, now that you mention it, but not the drink at the bar or anything afterwards. What else?"

She tilted her head defiantly. "I told you about my apartment, and you suggested we go there. You seemed all right until we got into the car; then you suddenly slumped against me as I got behind the wheel. I decided to go anyway—" Her voice faded.

"And that's the last you remember?"

She said gravely, "Yes."

We sat quietly side by side. I said presently, "It doesn't make sense. Think hard. Can you remember anybody coming out from the Cabana, offering to help?"

She shook her head. I tried a fresh attack. "What about that guy they bounced off the walls? Was he really annoying you or was it an act to scrape an acquaintance with me?"

Before she could answer, the door opened and Knife came in. I said, "Don't you ever knock before entering a room?"

He said equitably, "Only on front doors." His back stiffened. "What the hell brings you back? Kent know you're here?"

"I'm not on the story," I evaded. "Kent gave me a few days off, so I dropped around to see the girl friend."

The Gail said abruptly, "If we're going, I ought to change. I won't be a minute." She left in a few long strides.

Knife waited until the door had closed, then observed, "I can't dope that babe. Here her old man practically gets his head chopped

off, and all she worries about is looking classy for her boy friend."
With an effort he recalled the business at hand. "We checked the
time you and the dame left the Club Cabana. The doorman places
it around twelve-ten. We got Dillon's death narrowed to between
eleven-thirty and one-thirty."

"Isn't that cutting it pretty fine?"

"Not fine enough," Knife rumbled. "Say he was killed at one and
you got over six hours before they found the stuff. You can't rightly
tell much after so long. Stomach contents all digested, body heat
gone. It's a hell of a mess."

I said, "Honest, Lieutenant, if it was me, I'd confess. I wouldn't
hold out on a pal. How did you say he died?"

"I didn't." Knife looked discouraged. "He was strangled with
a wire."

He denied finding either the wire or the revolver from which two
bullets had been fired into the lawyer's already dead body. About
fingerprints, he admitted nothing except that some had been ob-
tained.

"How did you make out on the test of grease from the cars you
rounded up?"

He grimaced. "No dice. They all tested the same."

"What brings you back then? Don't tell me you're still questioning the family."

"Naw. I finished with them screwballs long ago. Jeez, ain't the
old lady a pip, though?" He yawned. "She was telling the truth all
right—anyways, mostly. Her alibi checks. We're working on the
blackmail angle now."

"Not Antoine St. Arles?"

"Nope." He smiled with secret satisfaction. "We got a much better
lead, though she musta nicked him for plenty, too."

"Five will get you ten it has something to do with the missing
picture," I bargained.

"For a snoop you ain't so dumb," he chuckled. He pushed himself
out of the chair. "I guess the boys are about finished up front. I
better look."

"Hunting more fingerprints?"

"Nope. We're searching the joint for some kind of hidden
papers."

"Sounds goofy to me."

"Me, too. But Osmond wants the joint searched, so we're searching it. The way the library was tossed around, maybe the killer got
scared off before he was finished hunting."

A plainclothes dick entered. He shook his head at Knife's unvoiced question.

"Take this one next." Knife jerked his head at me. "Better wait some place else, Phelps."

I strolled out into the hall and loafed at the foot of the landing. Presently the voices of Veronica and Laura Todd in quiet conversation drifted down. They walked downstairs and went toward the sitting room. There was a second of silence, probably when Veronica discovered what was going on, then a yelp of indignation.

Knife's voice said, "We got a warrant to do this, lady, so don't make no trouble."

Veronica shrilled, "I don't want your men in my room, Lieutenant Knife. Mr. Dillon did not have access to it."

The eruption must have been Knife exploding and was followed by ominous quiet and the slam of a door as the women retreated upstairs. A little while later Knife and the three dicks clumped after them, I suppose to Dillon's bedroom. I went back to the sitting room.

It would have required an expert to detect traces of the search. I sat down and waited for the Gail. It seemed to me she was taking her time about changing.

When the Gail finally entered, I complained, "You're certainly no quick change artist. I almost fell asleep."

She said, "I'm sorry, Chet. I couldn't resist the temptation of a bath."

I watched while she went over to a folding bar and hauled out bottles and glasses. She was tall as girls go, five-six or seven, I estimated, including high heels. Her head came up to my chin, and I'm a full six feet. Her figure was good, too, lithe and with long, free-swinging legs suggestive of grace and even strength. Granting that her father would have no reason to be chary of her, she appeared physically qualified to do the job.

I said, "I don't drink so early in the day. This is a special occasion."

"Special in what way?"

"It's been years since I've been chased by fatal blondes," I told her. "On the level, is that your own apartment? You can kid me, but the cops will find out quickly enough."

"You saw my bag. What do you think?"

"Since you ask me, I'll tell you. You're covering up for somebody, maybe Raymond. If it's his place, Knife will need at least ten minutes to discover it. Why make yourself out a tramp and let that slob get away with his filthy cracks?"

She was bent over the bar. "It's my apartment," she repeated stubbornly. "I rented it. I even signed a lease as Clarice Dill."

"I don't believe you."

She faced me, head erect. Her green eyes flared with contempt. "I'm so sorry to disappoint you. It's my apartment. Would you like to know what I use it for?"

"No. I'm convinced. I guess I'm still an adolescent at heart." I walked over to her, put my arms around her waist, pulled her close against me and kissed her savagely. She twisted out of my arms. I leered in imitation of Knife. "Did you like that?"

"I loved it." She laughed shakily, and rumpled my hair. "You just won't believe I'm a fallen woman, will you, darling?"

I couldn't help my sheepish grin. "What happened to our drinks?"

She asked, "Scotch?"

I shuddered. "Anything but." I settled for brandy.

She poured two man-sized hookers into snifter glasses. "Chaser?"

"Only in a small way," I said modestly.

She looked puzzled; then her brow cleared and she laughed, a deep throaty sound. "You'd be fun to know if we didn't have this between us," she observed.

"If you'd come clean we wouldn't have anything between us."

She frowned and tossed her yellow hair. I said, "This joint gives me the creeps. Put on your bib and we'll go punch some doorbells."

"I'm ready now."

I almost collided with Morgan at the front door. Annoyance spread over his face as he recognized me. I said, "Hello, fancy meeting you again."

He said with asperity, "I might say the same to you." He looked beyond me at the Gail. "Do you think it's wise to be seen in public with this man?"

She said, "I'll decide for myself what's wise." There was loathing and a touch of fear in her voice.

He appeared taken aback. "As your attorney I am merely—"

"You're not my attorney."

"Your mother's attorney, if you wish," he conceded. "This man is a reporter and a suspect in the eyes of the police as well. Entirely apart from the dictates of good taste, you are compromising your own safety by appearing with him."

I decided to take a hand. "You were Dillon's law partner, Mr. Morgan, and must have had some knowledge of his shady deals even if you weren't a party to them. How come you aren't a suspect, too?"

"You are skirting the edge of slander, young man."

"Make it libel and you'll be talking to an expert. I'm not trying to be fresh. I simply want to point out that we're all tarred with the same brush. You knew Dillon, and I'm his daughter's friend. There's no more or less reason to suspect one than the other of us." I produced a pencil. "Would you care to give me for publication an account of your whereabouts last night?"

He said stiffly, "I have made my statement to the police." He brushed by me. "If you will excuse me, I have an appointment with Mrs. Dillon."

I waited out front while the Gail brought her car from the garage. She said dreamily as I got in, "I want a drink, then another drink, then about five more drinks."

I said, "I'll settle for a pitcherful of Sidecars."

# CHAPTER 9

AS I RECALL, the original idea had been to imbibe a few quick jolts of liquid refreshment, with perhaps a touch of more solid nourishment, after which I firmly intended to go downtown and spread before Kent the crumbs of information I had picked up. Along about the third Sidecare, however, I decided I would stick to my role of lone wolf a bit longer.

I said, "You know, it's wonderful how a man's viewpoint will clarify if he sits down calmly and reasons stuff out."

We were sitting together, cozy and intimate, in a booth affair. She said, "Mm," and snuggled closer to my shoulder.

I said, "It's a crying shame, that's what it is, the way you're shoved around."

She said, "Drink your drink."

I got me a new idea. At the rate she was lapping up Sidecars on Kent's money, he was entitled to more than an anguished scream when I presented the bill. Get her oiled enough, and who knows what secrets might not come sliding down the runway. I said with enthusiasm, "Let's have another!"

"We haven't finished these," she objected.

"The hell with them. We need fresh ones."

Along about the third booth or the fourth—these places all look alike—Murphy from the Examiner appeared at my elbow. He peered under the table and asked where was Kent. I said I didn't know and cared less, which seemed to strike Murphy as a very funny remark.

I said, very dignified, "What's so funny?"

"You are, you boiled owl. What's Kent going to do without his stooge when they clap you in the can?"

"I'll show you who's a stooge," I rebutted.

I fished in my pocket and dug up a nickel. I crooked a finger at Murphy. He followed me to a telephone and waited while I got Kent on the wire.

I said, "Mr. Kent, will you settle a bet? There is some question of my standing. A says I am your stooge. B says I am not. I'm B. What am I?"

"You're a drunken, incompetent lout. Where are you?"

"No hedging now," I insisted. "What am I?"

"You're fired."

I said, "Thank you very much. I herewith tender my resignation." I hung up.

"Well, what did he say?" Murphy inquired.

I led the way back to our booth. I said to the Gail, "Come on; let's move along."

Murphy barred the way. "Can't take it, huh?" he crowed.

"You are greatly mistaken, sir," I chided. "You are looking at the three-time state champion taker." I pulled back my arm. "How are you at taking?"

I was greatly chagrined at being hit first. I am a firm believer in always hitting the other man first, because in a certain percentage of cases it is the end of the debate, especially if you hit him hard enough. When he sidestepped my return, I realized my timing was a little off, so I tackled him around the knees. Once down, it was a simple matter to bang his head decisively against the floor a few times.

My head cleared wonderfully from this healthful exercise, but we were heaved ·out just the same, I in injured silence, Murphy swearing he would sue me for assault with intent to kill, and the Gail kicking, biting, and gouging in vicious fury. It took all my strength to restrain her long enough for Murphy to rereat down the street.

We didn't stay long at the next place either, because there the Gail started a riot with a big Swede wench she claimed was trying to pick me up, when as a matter of fact I only bought her one drink out of ordinary civility. Back on the sidewalk, I brushed off my coat and said, "This is very monotonous. Cannot we find a haven where the milk of human kindness flows more freely?"

She asked suspiciously, "Where?"

"My hotel, the Beverly-Carlton. Kent keeps a couple of rooms there for us, just for appearances' sake, because he never sleeps any place but in the bed of a press."

"Well—anything to get away from those fat harpies."

We picked up a quart of rye at a package store. The drinks we had already absorbed had put a razor edge on the Gail's temper. All the way to the hotel I listened to a vivid account of what would happen if I sidled up to any more female barflies. By the time we arrived I was practically sober.

Her monologue was interrupted only momentarily when the attendant at the hotel took over her car for parking. She picked right up again as we entered the lobby and walked toward the elevators.

"The trouble with you, Chet Phelps, is that you're the type women pamper. Just because—"

The words died on her lips as the elevator door opened and half a dozen people from behind swept us into the car.

I said cheerfully, "Eleven." I turned to the Gail. "As you were saying, honey chile—"

The chalky whiteness of her face was a mask of blank terror. I followed her gaze over my shoulder and with an effort focused on the features of the man pressing against my back.

He said, "Hiya, pal."

I said without enthusiasm, "Hello, Jerry." I looked around for Roy and found him wedged between two jeweled ladies conversing loudly over his head.

Jerry and Roy followed us out, as I had expected they would. I introduced the Gail with false cordiality. "Have a drink with us, boys," I invited.

Color had drained back into the Gail's face. She said, "Sure, why not?"

We moved slowly down the carpeted hall to my room. Kent's was across the hall.

I put the key in the lock, turned it and pushed the door open, moving ahead to throw the light switch. A split second before the room flooded with light, something hard shoved against my side.

A voice said, "Reach high."

The Gail screamed. From behind me an arm reached over and chopped down viciously. The sound of a gun going off roared in my ear as I was knocked aside and sent sprawling.

I scrambled to my feet. The brief scuffle was already over. The Gail was huddled against the door. On the floor, just inside the sill, a man lay stretched out on his face. Jerry bent over him, one hand still clutching a wicked-looking blackjack. A few feet from the body lay the gun.

Roy said calmly, "You shouldn't have hit him so hard." He closed the door as running feet sounded along the corridor.

Jerry straightened up. "The bastard shot me," he said, outraged, holding up his left hand to show a streak of blood across the wrist.

Roy looked at me reproachfully. I shrugged, went over to the Gail and helped her to a chair. She was beyond speech. Fists pounded on the door.

"What's the trouble in there?"

Roy opened the door a crack. "No trouble at all, friend," he said evenly. "Just a little accident. Forget it."

Jerry struggled out of his coat, dropped it on the bed and went into the bathroom without haste. I made soothing sounds at the Gail, who grabbed my hand. Roy dropped his coat alongside Jerry's, stooped and picked up the gun. With his toe he turned over the man on the floor and studied his face.

"Ever see him before?" The question was collective.

I said, "No." The Gail shook her head.

Roy shrugged and dragged the inert figure to its feet. He called to Jerry over the sound of running water, "Hey, let's bring this punk to before the house dick shows up."

Jerry came out of the bathroom in his shirtsleeves. "Goddam it," he wailed, "I gotta dress my own wound, don't I? What kind of hospitality do you call this?" Still grumbling, he helped drag the man into the bathroom.

I picked up the wrapped bottle from the floor, opened it and poured two big hookers into tumblers from the dressing table. After she had emptied one of them, the Gail stammered, "He—he's not dead?"

"Naw, just sapped," I said with hollow cheerfulness. My knees felt wobbly. The telephone trilled insistently.

Roy came out, and ordered, "Answer it. Say it was an accident. Your friend was cleaning his gun and it went off. Nobody hurt."

I nodded and, in response to the desk clerk's excited yelp, repeated what I had been told, laughing off his offer of a doctor. I hung up on his demand for details. I shed my coat, helped the Gail remove hers.

The bathroom door opened, and Jerry and Roy came out, each holding one arm of a sullen-faced youth. He was back from dreamland, if a trifle unsteady on his legs. They dropped him into the other easy chair.

Roy, still taking charge, said, "Make us all drinks." He took the drinks as I poured them, and shoved one into the punk's hand. Knuckles rapped on the door. I looked at Roy, who nodded. He and Jerry sat on the edge of the bed, sipping their drinks. I opened the door. A burly, blue-jowled specimen of house dick pushed in, his right hand buried deep in his jacket pocket.

"What the hell goes on here?" he rasped.

I spread my hands and waited for Jerry. He waved his glass with the scratched hand and chortled.

"Had myself a little accident, pal," he apologized.

The house dick, snorting his disbelief, faced me. "You know these people, Mr. Phelps?"

"Sure, old friends of mine."

The dick returned to Jerry. "I suppose you was cleaning your gun. That's how it always happens, don't it?"

Jerry appeared astonished. "You certainly guessed it," he conceded, his head wagging in admiration.

"Let's have a look at it."

Jerry obediently held up his wrist. The dick's lips curled with scorn. "I mean the gun. Hand it over."

The dick flinched as Jerry suddenly reached in his back pocket and brought out a card case. He extracted a gun permit and allowed' the dick to inspect it.

"Jerry Candle," he read. "What's your business?"

"I'm a private investigator," Jerry said easily.

The dick tossed the permit back to Jerry. "You better get rid of these people, Mr. Phelps," he said abruptly. "And make it soon." He turned on his heel and slammed out.

I perched on the arm of the Gail's chair. "Don't mind me, boys," I snarled. "I only live here."

Nobody bothered to answer. Jerry picked up the phone, asked for room service and ordered two quarts of rye, glasses, cracked ice, a dozen bottles of ginger ale.

The Gail was rapidly beginning to feel better, maybe from the liquor. She said, "Is this a private party, or will it suit you gentlemen if Chet and I stay?"

Jerry hung up, grinning. "Stick around, sister," he advised. "We're going to have lots of fun."

The punk said dryly, "I bet."

"Me, too," I agreed. I walked across the room and retrieved my hat from the corner by the closet where it had apparently been kicked when I fell. It was a dirty and trampled mess. As I came erect, I thought I caught the punk watching me with more than casual interest. I brushed off the hat with my sleeve, adjusted its shape, tried it on. Definitely, it was too small for me. With that realization something in my mind clicked. I turned to the punk.

"What were you looking for when we came in?"

The punk shrugged and looked at the tips of his shoes. I dangled the hat at arm's length.

"Is this what you were after?"

He raised his eyes and regarded the hat just beyond his reach, as though seeing it for the first time.

Roy demanded with sudden interest, "Lemme see that."

I gave him the hat. Jerry moved over to his side. Roy turned the hat in his fingers, felt its quality, looked inside. He said, "Hey, this ain't yours. The initials in here are M.A.C."

"Sure," I said. "Mac. That's what the boys call me for a gag." I could cheerfully have kicked myself.

Jerry called, "Hey, punk, is this what you wanted?"

The punk made a derisive noise.

"Well," I vowed, "I'm going to find out even if I have to knock it out of him."

The punk rose slowly. Roy said, disgusted, "Keep your shirt on, pal, or you'll have the whole police force in here." The punk, expressionless, sat down again. Roy slid off the bed, went to the telephone, and gave the operator a number in a voice too low for me to hear.

There was a knock on the door, and a scared-looking bellboy skittered in with a trayful of glasses and ice. Behind him, another boy brought the whiskey and ginger ale. Before I could get my wallet out, Jerry had given the first boy a twenty-dollar bill and waved them both away. They bolted.

At the phone, Roy said loudly, "Lemme talk to Firelli. This is Roy Meade." While he waited, he winked at the punk, who turned pale and stirred in his chair.

Roy said, "That you, Firelli? Roy Meade. Yeah, fine, thanks. Say, I'm up here in Phelps' room at the Beverly-Carlton. Yeah, Phelps, the reporter. We got one of your punks here been cutting a few capers. Naw, nothing like that. Just playful."

He listened for a few seconds, smiling broadly. "That's fine," he said finally. "We'll be expecting you. Room Eleven Twenty-eight.

Don't bother knocking. Walk right in." He hung up, strolled over to the dresser and started to peel the seal from one of the new whiskey bottles.

The punk spoke suddenly. "I got to get out of here."

Roy said lightly, "What·the hell, pal, you're just·as well off in here as outside, now. What's your name, pal?"

The punk licked his lips. "Lugoni. Jack Lugoni. Are you really Roy Meade?" His mouth twisted.

Roy grinned his agreement.

We sat drinking for about twenty minutes before the door opened again. Osmond came in and, a step behind him, Firelli. Osmond rumbled a greeting and looked at the punk, who got up hastily and let the Commissioner have his chair. Firelli closed the door and leaned against it, saying nothing. He gave no sign of recognizing Lugoni, who moved over to the window and turned his back to the room.

Roy said, "Hello, gents. Hello, Firelli. Have a drink."

Firelli said curtly, "No."

From the chair, Osmond wheezed, "I'll have one." He chuckled. "Not supposed to drink, but what the hell, you only live once." Firelli did not move from the doorway.

Jerry entreated, "For the Lord's sake, sit down."

Firelli said, "No."

Osmond smote his thigh with a heavy palm. "Damn it," he roared, "sit down." He turned to me. "Give him a chair, sonny."

I took one of the two straight chairs from between the windows and carried it over to Firelli. "Thanks," he acknowledged, sitting down without haste. He took off his hat and flung it on the bed. I perched on the arm of the Gail's chair. I felt fine, a little drunk, but very pleased with myself. Roy bustled around with drinks, which Firelli refused again with a shake of his head.

Osmond sipped his drink, grunting with pleasure. He dug a huge cigar from his vest and clamped it between his teeth. The act served as a signal, because in a few minutes the room was heavy with the smoke of cigar and cigarettes. Even Firelli relaxed long enough to take a cigarette from his silver case.

Osmond orated through a cloud of smoke. "I don't want nobody to get me wrong, by God. When this call came for Mr. Firelli, him and I happened to be having a little talk. Coming along was strictly my own idea."

Roy beamed. "Oh, sure. Glad you did, Commissioner." He sat down on the bed beside Jerry.

Osmond continued, "As Police Commissioner, I got a hard job. I got to keep the peace." He pointed the cigar at Roy. "I don't want no feuds breaking out in this town. It hurts business." He seemed suddenly aware of my presence. "I mean general business," he added lamely. He puffed on the cigar. "One murder is enough, by God."

The Gail quivered. I patted her shoulder.

Roy said virtuously, "Sure. Live and let live. My partner don't like to be shot up every time he walks in a room."

Osmond coughed, and remarked, "Aw, now."

Roy continued as though there had been no interruption, "We didn't come up here for trouble."

"What did you come for?" Firelli queried. His voice was cold and unafraid. "What are you after? This is my territory. I don't go downstate."

Jerry laughed in delight, got up and walked over to Lugoni at the window. He draped his arm over the punk's shoulder and whispered in his ear. Lugoni flung off the arm but did not move. Firelli watched them.

Roy said, "We started out for a little visit."

From the window Jerry amended, "A social visit."

Roy picked it up. "We wanted to see how things are run up here. We didn't count on having a pal mixed up in a murder rap and Jerry shot. The boys won't like it."

Firelli cut in, "Who's the pal?"

"Why, Phelps is," Roy said, surprised. "He's a particular pal."

Firelli said a short word.

Osmond interjected hastily, "Wait now. We can straighten this all out. There must be some mistake."

Firelli showed his teeth. He said, "I'll do my own talking." He faced Roy squarely. "You're trying to muscle in. This is my town. Nobody pins a murder on me in my own town."

Jerry remonstrated from the window in a voice heavy with sorrow. "I got shot. That's personal."

Firelli said, "All right, you got shot. I'm sorry. Jack had no call to do it. I'll take it up with him later."

"Do that," Roy agreed. "But in the meantime—"

"There ain't no meantime," Firelli declared viciously. "That's all there is to it. I sent Jack up here to look around because I think Phelps has been holding out. If you say he's your pal, then it's okay as long as him and you stick to your own private business. But leave me out of it. I don't like to be pushed around and I don't like to be ribbed."

Roy turned to Osmond. "Mr. Commissioner, I ask you man to man. What about this murder? Like you said, it hurts business. What hurts business upstate hurts it downstate."

Osmond squirmed. "Well, now, we got leads, but it's too early to say."

Roy said triumphantly. "See what I mean? With a thing like this, the whole city is on trial, kind of. And naturally, when my partner gets shot—why, it begins to look like some people are beyond control. Next another guy gets shot and then there's real trouble on your hands."

Osmond said, troubled, "I don't care for that. You can positively leave it to me. I guarantee to make everything right."

Firelli stood up. His eyes darted about venomously. He made an animal sound deep in his throat. He said, "You all keep out of this— every last damn one of you." His eyes passed over the sardonically grinning Roy, rested on the police chief. He said more quietly, "You, too, Osmond. I put you up there, and I can pull you down if I have to."

Osmond said, "By God." He sounded more hurt than angry.

---

# CHAPTER 10

---

**M**Y WRIST-WATCH on the bedside table said it was ten o'clock when I awoke. I phoned room service and ordered breakfast sent up, then asked the operator whether there had been any calls for me, and got a negative answer. It seemed advisable to call the Free Press for clarification of my current status.

Katie said, "Mr. Kent left word that you were a drunken you-know-what. He also said you were fired and to get the address where you wanted your check mailed."

"Fine. What else?"

She laughed. "He had to go to a Publishers' Alliance meeting at ten-thirty. In case you don't know, it's eleven-fifteen now and Wednesday. He said if you happened to be in the lobby of the Printing Arts Building at noon, he might possibly listen to one of your lousy alibis."

At ten minutes to twelve I took up a post commanding a view of the express elevator bank at the Printing Arts Building. Kent didn't appear, but the girls who passed were beautiful, so to kill time I practiced up on my leering. After a while the starter gave me a dirty look. I strolled over to him, and said out of the corner of my mouth, "Federal Bomb Squad. Don't worry; we have the building covered," and watched while he tried not to faint. I then resumed my leering.

At twelve-fifteen Kent emerged with J. Farthington Ashcroft, who wore white piping on his vest and owned the Examiner. He had Kent firmly by the elbow and seemed to be urging him to some course of action. Kent scowled as I hurried over, but gave no sign of recognition.

I mouthed breathlessly, "Mr. Kent, we just got a tip Gruffjub confessed to the Dillon—" I stopped in confusion as he gave me a terrible glare.

Ashcroft released Kent's elbow. He gulped, "Another time, then, perhaps, old man," and left the lobby at a trot, almost knocking down the starter, who tottered over to us.

"Wasn't that the man, sir?" he whined.

Kent frowned and walked away. I whispered, "Yeah, the beefy boy with the trimmed vest. If he ever shows up again, phone Headquarters." I caught up with Kent on the sidewalk.

I cleared my throat. "About Gruffjub—"

He said, "Never mind. I can imagine." He suddenly began to laugh. "What did you tell the starter?"

I confessed. He laughed all the way down to the corner, where he recalled he was still sore at me, but by then it was too late. He said, "That old humbug wanted me to lunch with him."

"I could do with a touch of food myself," I hinted.

"All right," he said largely. "We'll eat at the Marguaray."

The Marguaray, for all its fancy name, was a lunchroom around the corner from the Free Press building. We found two seats at the far end of the corner. Ginny gave the marble a perfunctory swipe with a damp cloth.

"What'll it be today?"

Kent studied the menu. "I'll have the special," he decided. "Meatballs and spaghetti."

I shuddered. "Bacon and eggs, as usual."

Kent said, "I believe we have traced the shirt and tie you found at Miss Dillon's apartment. They were purchased last week from a Main Street haberdasher by a man answering Dillon's general description. If you are ever called on to explain your possession of them—"

I groaned, "Ouch. Here's something I forgot to tell you. I also acquired a new hat at the apartment. My own was missing." I took off the hat and gave it to him. "What with one thing and another, it slipped my mind."

He scrutinized the hat gravely, noting the initials.

"Do you know any M.A.C.?"

I shook my head. "Wait until you hear the rest." I rapidly told him about Knife's search of the Dillon manse for blackmail documents, slid lightly over the interval at the various bars and concluded with the assault and powwow at the Beverly-Carlton. When I finished I glanced up. Ginny was standing over us, mouth agape.

Kent said irritably, "Go away and bring our food."

She stalked off in wounded dignity.

Kent resumed, "Then in your opinion the hoodlum came for the express purpose of recovering this hat?"

"I think so. I'm positive Firelli recognized it. So did the Gail."

Kent said, "What about your thug friends, Candle and Meade?"

Ginny said, "Oh, them kind always have poker faces."

I said, "Are you back? I would like to have my bacon and eggs."

She muttered, "Aw," and went off.

I said, "Why don't we hold our conferences in Woolworth's?"

Kent grunted, and we talked for a while about Firelli. Ginny came back with my food. "What did I miss?"

I said, "Nothing much. We can't decide whether Firelli came to get his punk or just to show Jerry and Roy he wasn't afraid of them."

Ginny said, "What happened to him?"

"Who?"

"The punk."

"He left with Jerry and Roy after a while."

"When did Miss Dillon leave?"

I said, "Uh—bring me the ketchup."

She piped, "You men," and flounced off.

"That was just for Ginny's benefit," I told Kent. "The Gail went home alone about a half hour later."

"She is an enigmatic creature," he mused.

"You're telling me? She slapped my face."

He said, "I don't like this new development of missing papers. It smacks of cheap melodrama. I like even less the business with Firelli and those men. How did they happen to be at our hotel?"

I said innocently, "You can search me. Coincidence, I guess."

He studied me over a forkful of spaghetti. "I wonder. Are you sure.you did not make contact with them despite my orders?"

I evaded the question. "Honest, I didn't look for them."

"You will end up by placing your head in a noose," he predicted.

I thought it advisable to change the subject. "Did Antoine call you?"

"No."

"I'll still bet she does."

He shook his head in disbelief. "Since you insist on meddling with this story, you may as well make yourself useful. See Raymond Dillon this afternoon and sound him out on his relationship with his father. I have an idea there was little love lost between the senior and junior Dillons."

"How am I supposed to persuade him to take down his back hair? He hates my guts."

"Your methods are unique. I wouldn't dream of interfering with them."

I ventured, "This hat is the best lead we've uncovered yet. It means something to Firelli and the Gail."

"No doubt," he conceded dryly, "but what?"

I shrugged. Ginny gave us our checks, thirty-five cents for Kent, fifty for me. As we parted, he said, "Report as soon as you have finished with young Dillon, but in no event later than five o'clock. And buy yourself a new hat. I'll take charge of this one."

I said, "Aye, aye, sir," and strolled off, hatless.

The proposed interview with Raymond struck me as strictly a gag designed to keep me occupied and out from under foot, but I knew better than to disobey a specific order. I bought a new hat, then dropped into a drugstore for cigarettes. I gave the clerk a quarter, and he handed me two pennies and a shiny new Jefferson nickel as change. I looked at the nickel, then at a row of three telephone booths against the wall. They were empty and inviting. I thought, What can I lose?

I thumbed through the directory, then stepped into one of the booths and dialed my number. A switchboard operator answered. I asked to be connected with Miss St. Arles. The operator said Miss St. Arles wasn't accepting calls.

I said frigidly, "This is Mr. Sanderson of Continental Airlines. We're checking back on a reservation. I'm sure Miss St. Arles will speak with me."

After a little delay a feminine voice said, "This is Miss St. Arles. Who did you say was calling?"

"Mr. Sanderson of Continental Airlines, Miss St. Arles," I

gargled. "About that reservation for a seat on the ten-forty plane to Chicago, I'm sorry, but we've had no cancellations for trip twelve and can't promise you a seat."

She exclaimed, "Wait a minute. Who placed the reservation?"

"One moment please," I put down the receiver, took the cigarettes from my pocket. I opened the package, extracted and lit a cigarette. I picked up the receiver. "Miss St. Arles? Sorry to keep you waiting." The reservation was placed by Mr. George Brown and came over the telephone. He said you were leaving town unexpectedly because of your health. He gave us your name and telephone number for our report."

She said in a choked voice, "Oh, yes, of course."

I went on pleasantly, "I hope it is nothing serious, Miss St. Arles. I'm frightfully sorry to disappoint you on trip twelve, but we do have a seat left for trip thirteen. May I book you for it? The trip skips the stop at—"

She said, No, I had better not make the reservation for the later plane until she spoke with George again. She was so mad her voice trembled, but I made her listen to a brisk sales talk on the advantages of going by Cincinnati until she practically slammed the receiver in my face.

Leaving the phone booth, I stopped at a display of brightly colored little jars and bought one for fifty cents, then continued on my way with a distinct feeling of having done my good deed for the day. I hailed a passing cab and rode to the Dillon manse. There was no cop on duty today. A maid answered my ring. She looked terrified and acted as though she were ready to slam the door in my face. I asked for Raymond Dillon and was reluctantly admitted to the foyer. A minute or two later Laura Todd came downstairs.

"Really, Mr. Phelps," she protested, "you might allow us a little peace."

I said, "I'm sorry, Miss Todd. Barging in like this isn't my idea. Mr. Kent wants me to interview your fiancé."

"Well—I'll ask him. Please wait in there." She indicated the room where I had been questioned by Knife.

I dropped my coat on one of the chairs, and settled myself to wait. It occurred to me that this small room, just off the foyer, would make an excellent hiding place at night for anybody who wanted to keep a watch on people entering or leaving the house.

Laura Todd returned with Raymond, who gave me a reluctant greeting. Raymond's manner was openly hostile, Laura's nervous and conciliatory. Obviously, she hoped by her presence to avert a bad scene.

He said stonily, "I understand you want to interview me."

"It's Mr. Kent's idea, not mine," I corrected. "But first I'd like, if possible, to change your impression of what happened Monday night. I give you my word I was in no condition to molest your sister."

Raymond said evenly, "You're a liar. You've known my sister for a year. You persuaded her to rent an apartment under an assumed name. If that isn't—"

"Raymond, please—" Laura put her hand on his arm. "Mr. Phelps, if you have any questions, please ask them."

"He's not going to like them any more than what I've already said," I warned, "but here goes." I addressed Raymond. "Were there any recent differences of opinion between you and your father?"

"No."

"When did you last see him?"

"Monday afternoon. I had packed my dinner clothes to take over to Miss Todd's. I went out into the hall, intending to let Mother know I was ready to leave. I heard a sound downstairs, looked, and saw my father enter the house. He went directly to the library."

I said, for lack of a better question, "Can you recall how he was dressed?"

"He had on a blue serge suit." He frowned. "Or an Oxford gray. I'm not sure. The light isn't good in the hall."

I said, startled, "Wait a minute. When he was found he was wearing a brown tweed."

"Yes."

"Did he frequently change in the late afternoon?"

Raymond said indifferently, "Sometimes."

I said, crestfallen, "Thank you," and got up. "I guess that's all."

The door opened and Morgan looked in. He was in a fine humor. He said, "Well, well. I fancied I heard voices and decided I had better investigate."

"Mr. Phelps is just leaving," Laura told him.

Morgan smiled at me as though we were the best of friends. "Which way are you going?"

"Downtown."

"Fine. I'll give you a lift."

I said, "Thanks," and thought, What now?

Morgan tapped my arm. "Ready?"

I nodded, and put on my coat.

Laura said, "Gail is upstairs. Shall I tell her—"

"Don't bother," I said gloomily. I mumbled a meaningless phrase of apology and followed Morgan to his car. He was still giving out with quantities of fellowship. "I freely admit I thought your account of having been drugged a feeble effort," he said with a disarming smile. "Since then I have reconsidered and am inclined to take your story more seriously." .

"You believe we were drugged?" I made no effort to conceal my surprise. "Coming from you, Firelli's lawyer—"

"Not quite so fast, I beg. I did not mean to imply complete acceptance of the theory. A trial lawyer, you know, gets to be a bit of a medical man, too. Excessive alcoholic consumption can produce a mental lapse, for example."

Light dawned on me. "I get it now. You're outlining Firelli's defense in case Kent and I kick up a stink."

"You are a hard young man," Morgan observed wryly.

We passed Swanson Boulevard and sidled into Main Street traffic. "You can drop me at the next light," I directed.

"Are you bound for another appointment?"

"No."

"Why not come up to my place for a quick drink? There are a few things I'd like to discuss with you."

"Good enough. I'm not due downtown until five."

We left Main Street and headed southeast. He began again after a short pause, "I fancied you had the impression yesterday that Mr. Hendrickson accorded me special courtesy."

"Frankly, yes."

His lips twitched. "I hope you do not subscribe to the fiction that courtroom opponents must be sworn enemies."

I said, "I've been Mr. Kent's personal secretary for five years. The previous five I spent as a police reporter. I don't subscribe to any kind of fictions."

"Excellent. Then you will not be shocked to learn that, apart from our legal tilts, the district attorney and I enjoy a friendship predating his election to public office."

"You mean he let you tell your story in private?"

"Yes, but not solely on the grounds of friendship. The law grants to attorneys a certain immunity from questioning, since otherwise they might be compelled to testify against their clients. I cannot, it is true, cloak my own movements in privilege, but I am entitled to private explanation if what I have seen or been told places another person in jeopardy."

I stopped him. "One minute, Mr. Morgan. Police reporters pick up a smattering of law the way lawyers do of medicine. The right of privileged communications, as I understand it, covers only your actual clients."

"Yes, of course."

"And it goes only for what they tell you, not what you see. You can't watch a client commit a crime and supress your knowledge on the ground of privileged communication."

He said hastily, "No, no. Certainly not."

"Yet you said you were entitled to private explanation of what you had seen or been told."

"A slip of the tongue." He looked flustered. "When a lawyer explains a point to a layman, he is frequently guilty of oversimplification."

I said, "All right. Don't simplify. Veronica Dillon wasn't your client last Monday. Firelli was and is. Are you withholding something he told you because it is privileged?"

Morgan laughed heartily. "Really, a good trial lawyer was lost in you. No, I am not withholding anything. I have merely been. pointing out to you the various reasons why Mr. Hendrickson deemed it advisable to question me privately."

The car drew up before .a small apartment house. Morgan leaned across me and opened the door. "Better wait for me in the lobby," he advised. "I'll find a parking place and be with you in a. minute."

I walked inside, noting the absence of a doorman. The lobby was furnished in quiet good taste very different from the garish splendor of the Albermarle. There was no switchboard, but instead a simple house phone system over which the elevator operator could announce guests before taking them upstairs.

Morgan came along almost immediately. "Don't look for anything fancy," he cautioned. "I lead a simple bachelor life." He turned to the boy. "Any messages?"

The boy said, "No sir, Mr. Morgan."

"Do you have hotel service here?" I inquired.

"No. A woman comes in mornings and cleans up."

We got off at the fourth floor. Morgan led the way down the corridor and inserted a key into the lock of his door. He said, as he pushed the door open, "What will you have—Scotch or rye?"

I looked straight into the muzzle of a revolver. I said, "Make mine a short beer."

# CHAPTER 11

A NTOINE ordered, "Shut the door." She shifted the gun a few inches to point at Morgan's mid section. As though in a dream, he obeyed. He opened his mouth to speak, but no sound emerged. He simply stared, fascinated.

I crossed the room slowly, conscious of the gun following my movements, and sat down in an easy chair so placed that Antoine could not cover me and Morgan simultaneously. She jiggled the gun around nervously. "Get up out of there."

Morgan pleaded, "Antoine—for heaven's sake. Have you lost your mind?"

She backed up still further, against the far wall. "Get over by him."

Morgan shrugged, and walked slowly over to where I was sitting. I cursed him under my breath. Apart, we had a chance to catch her off guard, but now she had us both covered nicely. As though gathering courage from my proximity, Morgan tried to reason with her again. She menaced him with the gun, and he fell silent.

I thought, If she hasn't started firing already, she'll lose courage the longer it's postponed. I said very quietly. "Better think it over, Antoine. Guns make a lot of noise when they go off. You're flirting with the death house."

Morgan caught his breath in a quick sob of fear. I continued talking. "Before you can fire two shots, one of us will have you. It's four flights to the street, and an elevator boy is in the lobby. Is it worth the gamble?"

"Damn you, shut up," she screamed.

Morgan spoiled it again. "Phelps—don't," he threatened. "You're making things worse." He collapsed weakly on the arm of my chair, thus providing her with a target impossible to miss. He began to babble. "Antoine—I swear to you—I don't know what this is all about."

His evident terror only increased her fury. "So you thought you could scare me out of town?" Her voice mounted higher and higher. In a few moments, I knew, she would have worked herself up to the sticking point.

I thought, I got him into this, I've got to get him out. I cried sharply, "Look out!" Her eye shifted momentarily, and I lunged out of the chair. She brought the gun up, and fired three shots in rapid succession as I tripped and sprawled on the floor at least a good two feet from her. Behind me I heard Morgan moan and a thud as his body hit the floor. I clutched my belly and made horrible strangling noises, half closing my eyes.

Antoine stood over me for a long moment, then, still clutching the gun, ran to the door. I lay perfectly still until I heard the door slam. Then I jumped after her, lost precious seconds over the unfamiliar lock, and raced down the hall. It was deserted.

Even as I turned back I wondered why she had been so bold and why the shots had raised no alarm. Then I realized these were small apartments occupied by business couples. At this hour there probably wasn't another person on the whole floor and few in the entire building.

I hurried across the room to where Morgan lay on the floor, face down, alongside the chair. I turned his body over, mechanically felt for the heart beat, found it regular and strong. Puzzled, I searched for a wound, and finally located a tear halfway up his right coat sleeve. I propped him up and stripped off his topcoat and jacket. Under his shirtsleeve I saw a tiny smear of blood.

I picked him up and laid him, still unconscious, on a couch placed between the windows. I ripped off the sleeve, went into the bathroom, found iodine and bandage in the medicine closet. With a dampened towel I washed his arm and discovered only a long scratch, where the bullet had furrowed the skin. I put iodine on the cut. Morgan jerked, his eyelids fluttered, but he did not come to.

I went into the bedroom, found the telephone and dialed Kent's private number. When I heard his cool, dry voice I felt as though a load had been lifted from my shoulders. I wasted no time over preliminaries. I said, "This is Chet. I'm at Morgan's apartment. He was just shot by Antoine, not badly, only nicked."

Kent fussed. "Really, Mr. Amstrutter, I am a very busy man."

I said, "I can't call back. He's out from fright, but he'll come to any minute. Give me a tip on how to handle this. I had to let Antoine escape, but there's been no alarm yet."

Kent said pompously, "There are many demands on my time, sir. If I were to attend every committee meeting to which I am invited—"

I said, "The address is Fourteen Twenty-eight Underhill Drive. I'll tell the elevator boy we're expecting a caller, so you won't have to give your name."

Kent said in a voice of weary acquiescence, "Very well, Mr. Amstrutter, I will come down at once, provided no action of any sort will be determined upon before my arrival."

"I'll keep him quiet," I promised.

Kent purred, "I hope the committee members will be in a proper frame of mind, Mr. Amstrutter." He hung up.

I returned to find Morgan raised up on his good elbow. He gave me a dazed look, then sank back with a moan. The skin of his cheeks was yellow and beaded with little drops of perspiration.

"Don't try to move, old man," I shouted in alarm, and was rewarded by a groan.

He rolled his eyes fearfully. "What happened?"

"You've been shot."

He almost fainted again. "Am—am I badly hurt?"

"Don't talk now." I bent down, gathered him in my arms as carefully as though he had glass corners, and staggered into the bedroom. He permitted me to undress him and put him to bed. When he caught sight of his bandaged arm, he shuddered and his teeth chattered. I thought it advisable to forestall any demand for a doctor. "The bullet didn't lodge in your arm," I explained. "You've had a bad shock. I've seen men die of shock after a gunfight."

I went outside, poured a thimbleful of Scotch for him and a hooker of rye for myself. I downed the rye, brought the Scotch inside and fed it to him, drop by drop.

He whimpered, "You're a good lad, Phelps." He licked his lips. "Do you suppose I could have a drop more?"

"Better not," I said judiciously. "Try to rest. I'll be outside if you need me."

"You won't leave me?"

I reassured him, and tiptoed out of the room. I poured myself a fresh drink, realized I was still wearing my topcoat and shed it. I found the house phone near the outer door and informed the elevator boy that Mr. Morgan was expecting a visitor shortly.

I passed the time until Kent's arrival glancing through the illustrations in some back issues of Esquire I unearthed. My mind touched briefly on the explanation Kent would demand, and I poured myself another drink in a hurry. I wondered where Antoine had gone after presumably killing two men. From that I passed on to where I would go if I were a horse, and decided on the Kentucky Derby, which was no help. The doorbell rang. I leaped to answer it.

Kent strode by me, closed the door. "Where is he?"

"In the bedroom, recovering from shock. He's afraid to call a doctor and is stoically bearing his pain alone—with me standing by, just in case."

Kent put down his hat and eased out of his coat. "Why did she shoot him?"

"She shot at me, too."

"Never mind about you. Why did she shoot him?"

"Maybe she killed Dillon—I think."

Kent opened his mouth, then closed it in a tight line. He put his hands behind his back and crackled: "Look at me, Chet."

I looked at him.

He said, "Why did she shoot him?"

"Because I called her up after I left you and pretended to be a Mr. Sanderson of the Continental Airlines."

He nodded. "Go on."

I said sorrowfully, "I was merely trying to be helpful."

"I don't doubt it. What did you tell Miss St. Arles?"

"That the Continental had a plane reservation for her placed by a Mr. George Brown." I gathered a little confidence. "I didn't mention Morgan by name—not once. If she wanted to draw her own conclusions—" I met his eye. "That wasn't good, was it?"

He said, "No."

"I thought she would come running to you with the true story of what happened Monday night."

"Instead she tried to murder Mr. Morgan."

"Yes."

He said, "I will attend to you presently."

Morgan's voice called, "Phelps. Who's out there?"

Kent walked into the bedroom, and sat at the foot of Morgan's bed. He said, "I am shocked, inexpressibly shocked. Why should Miss St. Arles wish to take your life?"

Morgan, plucking at the covers, shook his head.

Kent smiled. "Come now, Mr. Morgan. We can hardly print the news of an almost fatal assault without offering a reason, no matter how far-fetched."

"She didn't mean to kill me. It was an accident."

"I fear you owe us an explanation, Mr. Morgan," Kent insisted. "You must not forget that Chet's life was also endangered."

Morgan said, "I need a drink."

I brought it, a big one this time. He took the glass, swallowed, and said wearily, "She was jealous. For some reason—I have no idea why —she must have thought I was planning a reconciliation with my wife."

Kent pressed his advantage. "Whereas you had promised to marry Miss St. Arles after you were divorced?"

"Yes." Morgan eyed us to judge the effect of his revelation. On me it was colossal.

"Actually, I have not even remotely considered such a move," he went on. "My wife and I separated many years ago. She is not even in the city. I—I have endeavored to keep this early marriage from my present associates." He darted a covert glance at Kent.

Kent gazed at the ceiling. "You ask me to believe Miss St. Arles' jealousy was wholly independent of factors arising from your partner's death?"

"Yes."

"I cannot. Casual jealousy may prompt tearful scenes, even moderate violence, not gunplay. You must do better, sir."

Morgan began to bluster. Then he tried pleading and profuse restatement. When he finally stopped, exhausted, Kent continued inexorably, "You refuse to be frank with me. Would you like to have me guess at the true state of affairs?"

Morgan lay back and closed his eyes.

Kent said, "Miss St. Arles transferred her allegiance from Jeffrey Dillon to you in the hope of marriage. But upon the death of Mr. Dillon, she felt the situation had changed. You no longer needed her intimate knowledge of Jeffrey's affairs."

"It's not true."

"I did not say it was," Kent admitted placidly. "I am simply guessing at the lady's mental processes. For reasons best known to herself, Miss St. Arles considers you a dangerous person. She learned, somehow, that your affection for her could no longer be counted upon. Fearful of what she knew or suspected, she jumped blindly from the fact that you no longer needed her to the conclusion that her own life was imperiled. Therefore she sought to shoot you before you could shoot her."

Morgan essayed a sickly smile. "You're talking nonsense."

"I disagree. You are a clever man, Mr. Morgan. Would it not be wiser to tell us the grounds for Miss St. Arles' fears than to have me guess further?"

Morgan gestured surrender. "After Jeffrey phoned me last Monday night, I determined to see him immediately rather than wait until eleven-thirty. I called back within a half-hour and, receiving no answer, assumed he had stepped out momentarily. I rang up Antoine and asked her to come here to guard against the possibility of my missing Jeffrey should he anticipate the appointment hour. I drove to his house. It was empty and locked. When I returned, Antoine told me there had been no word from him. I phone again and this time reached him."

"Impossible," Kent exclaimed. "Unless both she and Raymond lied, Miss St. Arles didn't leave her apartment until about ten-thirty. If you found her awaiting you here, either you did not leave until almost ten-thirty, or you left much earlier and were gone ominously long for a round trip to and from a deserted house."

"I don't know what you're driving at."

"Simply this: You held no phone conversation with Jeffrey Dillon at eleven. It is precluded on other grounds as well. Had Miss St. Arles heard you talking with your partner, she would not entertain the notion that you killed him."

Morgan drew a quick breath. He said, "I am forced to put myself at your mercy. I didn't speak with Jeffrey after his first call at nine-thirty. Antoine took the message before I returned. Jeffrey wanted me to know he might be a little delayed. I sent Antoine home when Jeffrey still hadn't shown up at one o'clock. The next morning, when I learned he had been killed, I was afraid my visit to his house during the evening might be misconstrued. I called Antoine and suggested we pretend I had been here to take Jeffrey's second call. I didn't realize until now how the request might sound to her." His eyes were humble.

Kent ignored the implied plea.

"At what time did you in fact reach the Dillon house?"

"Ten-thirty. I had talked with Antoine just before ten, and she assured me she would leave at once. Raymond arrived meanwhile and delayed her."

"What was the nature of your business with Mr. Dillon at such a late hour?"

Morgan did not hesitate. He said promptly, "Jeffrey phoned to tell me that he intended to give to the federal attorney certain documents damaging to my client Mr. Firelli."

Kent frowned. "You made the appointment in the hope of dissuading him?"

"Yes. I tried to convince him that he had nothing to fear from Mr. Firelli. He calmed somewhat, and in the end promised to do nothing until he had seen me."

Kent stated not as a question, but as a fact, "You, of course, made no mention of such documents to Mr. Hendrickson."

Morgan echoed, "Certainly not. To do so would be tantamount to casting suspicion on my client who, I am positive, had nothing whatever to do with the crime. Jeffrey's fears were induced by his phobia —nothing more."

Kent held up his hand. "One moment. You claim to be positive of Firelli's innocence. Does your assurance spring from knowledge or conjecture?"

Morgan said reluctantly, "Conjecture—naturally."

"I see. For the time being, Mr. Morgan, the Free Press will make no mention of this afternoon's affray."

Morgan said fulsomely, "Thank you. Thank you very much."

Kent rose, brushed a speck of lint from his trousers. He said, "You have only Miss St. Arles' word for Jeffrey's call and, in fact, for her presence here while you were away, have you not?"

Morgan stared. He said, "Yes."

"Could she have gone directly from her apartment to the Dillon home, stayed briefly and then come here before you got back?"

Morgan gave this visible thought. "Yes, just barely. I had to walk to the garage for my car, and returned it to the garage again before I came upstairs."

Kent said, "Have you any idea where Miss St. Arles secured a gun?"

Morgan flushed. "Jeffrey gave her a small revolver several years ago. It's little more than a toy."

"I see. I will not trouble you further." Amusement danced briefly in Kent's eyes. "If you rest for the balance of the day, by tomorrow you should be fully recovered. Good afternoon."

We rode the elevator in silence. The silence thickened as we reached th sidewalk. Without a glance at me, Kent started to walk down the street. I fell into step beside him.

Kent followed Underhill Road to. its intersection with Forrest, turned into Forrest and started walking briskly in the general direction of Main Street, some two miles off. I knew he detested walking, but I said nothing. He kept his eyes front, seemingly oblivious to my presence at his side. We covered three blocks in this fashion. At Forrest and Westfield we had to wait for a light to change.

Kent said without preamble, "You are spared a man's blood on your conscience only because Miss Arles' aim was not better."

I said, "Well—I pulled a jackass stunt, but I'll bet now Morgan really has been in touch with his wife."

"No doubt. However, if he were lying dead at this moment—" The light changed and he left the sentence hanging in mid-air. He crossed the street.

I hastened after him. I said tentatively, "Well, it brought him out into the open."

He said explosively, "Firelli was right. I should have kept you on a chain. One murder has already been attempted as a result of your efforts. I shudder in contemplation of what may yet come."

We reached Forrest and Haven.

"To hell with fresh air," I suggested. "Let's sit down some place and figure this out over a drink."

He said dubiously, "I should return to the plant."

"What for? They'll vote me a medal for combing you out of their hair for a few hours." I reached in my pocket. "Look, I got a present for you. I almost forgot it."

Kent asked suspiciously, "What is it?"

"A new kind of nail wax. It's nonskid and pliant. We'll go have a drink and you can try it out. I know just the place. It's called the Circus Bar."

Kent's face lit up with pleasure. He hailed a cab and, even before it started rolling, had the package open and was studying the directions for using the wax. He was concentrating so hard that I knew he scarcely heard the report of my interview with Raymond or Jeffrey Dillon's preference for brown tweed suits to be murdered in.

# CHAPTER 12

THE Circus Bar was a saloon adorned in the modern manner with posters and paraphernalia of the big top. I maneuvered Kent toward the bar, failed to spot Jeannette Ackley in the good-natured crowd, and veered off. Kent eyed me quizzically. "Are you looking for someone?"

I said, "No," and led the way to a table. "My cousin comes here once in a while," I volunteered, "and I thought she might be around."

Kent looked skeptical but made no comment. He ordered Scotch and soda for us, put the jar of nail wax on the table, then resolutely pushed it to one side. He said, "Connivance between Miss St. Arles and members of Mr. Dillon's family is too remote a possibility to merit serious consideration. Either Dillon was alive to be talked with at eleven or his voice was imitated."

According to the autopsy he didn't die until eleven-thirty at the earliest," I reminded him.                                             •

Kent brushed that aside. "When the discovery of a body has been long delayed, few coroners hesitate to draw on external evidence to help fix the time of death. Three people talked with the deceased after eleven; therefore, reasons the coroner, the man must have been alive at least until that time, and he so finds. No, we cannot consider the autopsy as substantiating the calls."

I said, "We've got Morgan in a tight spot. Having lied about speaking with Dillon, he could be lying all along the line. If we told Hendrickson—"

"He would laugh at us. The district attorney was sitting in my office when you called. He gave me to understand that Mr. Morgan had excellent reason for telling his story in private and, furthermore, the district attorney's office was satisfied with the explanation as given."

I said, "Yes. Morgan lectured me on privileged communication before we were slightly interrupted by the fireworks display."

Our drinks came and tasted as good as Scotch and soda can to a man who prefers rye. Kent fooled with the nail wax, declared, "I don't like the smell of those phone calls. They are no outright fiction, yet I cannot believe three people who knew Jeffrey's voice so well could have been taken in by an imitation."

I voiced the alternative, "Well, then, what's wrong with the old boy being alive at eleven?"

Kent said testily, "Everything." He swallowed, put down his glass. "I'd better let the paper know where we are." He fumbled in his pockets.

I gave him a nickel, commenting, "You have a statistical mind. What percentage of my salary do you suppose you've wheedled from me in the five years of these petty larceny tricks?"

He muttered, "Insufferable young puppy," but took the nickel just the same, and departed in search of a phone. I seized the opportunity to order a rye highball. I twisted around to face the bar, but got only a rear view of heads and legs. I decided it wouldn't do any harm to have my drink there and instructed the waiter to let me know when Kent returned.

Almost immediately I saw Jeannette at the core of a group of muscular young men. She wriggled free and flung herself into my arms.

She gurgled, "Where were you yesterday, Dick?"

"Dick?" I blinked. "Who's Dick?"

Her manner was reproachful. "I never forget a name. Yours is Dick Davis."

"Oh, yeah, sure," I acknowledged. "I didn't realize you meant me. What are you drinking?"

"Whatever you are. Make it a double Manhattan."

Kent appeared at my elbow, said, "I've been looking for you."

Jeannette said out of the side of her mouth, "Beat it, bum," and smiled at me sweetly.

I gulped. I said, "Hey, hey, this is my boss."

Jeannette hiccoughed gently, "My mistake. Any friend of Dick Davis is a friend of mine." She put out her hand. "Shake."

Kent accepted the hand gravely, and replied with great courtesy, "And any friend of Mr. Davis is truly a friend of mine. Won't you join us?"

I said, alarmed, "Oh, no, cousin Jeanney has to run along."

Jeannette said flatly, "You're bugs. I just got here."

Kent led the way back to our table. He helped Jeannette sit down, saying with a malicious smile, "I don't believe I caught your name, my dear."

"Jeannette Ackley. What's yours?"

"Jack London."

"I like Richard Harding Davis better for a name."

A tall, good-looking boy drifted past our table. He waved at Jeannette, kept on moving. I said to Kent, "Hold everything," and dived after him.

The boy turned at my tap on his shoulder, recognized me, and said with a sickly grin, "Do we have to do it again?"

I said, "No, let's just talk this time. I'll buy a drink."

Kent looked amused as we returned. He asked, "Another member of your family?"

Jeannette said, "Hiya, Raoul."

I shook my head warningly. "Remember last Monday night? This is the chap I was telling you about."

Kent took the cue. "Yes, of course. Won't you join us?"

The boy said, "Thanks, I don't care if I do." He was very frightened. The waiter took his order for beer.

I reminded him, "We traded a few friendly punches the other night, but it didn't wind up according to the script."

He grinned, still uneasily. "You're telling me?" He rubbed his scalp. "What did you hit me with—a safe?"

"No. I happened to catch you off balance. Then one of Firelli's men smacked you with a rubber blackjack."

Astonishment spread over his face. He said slowly, "No wonder I went out so cold. Why, them dirty, double-crossing bastards."

Kent had been listening closely. He said now, "You're a professional fighter, Mr.—"

"Langueste. Raoul Langueste, but I fight as Irish Ned. It don't sound so nancy. I'm still in the small-time."

Kent nodded. He said, "Don't be offended, Mr. Langueste, but isn't the Club Cabana a rather fast place for a struggling young fighter?"

Langueste said, "No offense. I was up there job hunting. One of their bouncers quit, and I was tipped off about the opening. Mr. Firelli told me to hang around and get the feel of the place. Later he come back and said there was a feller in the joint spoiling for trouble they might try me out on."

I said, "I'm beginning to get it."

"Yeah. He pointed out a girl he said was a society dame and lit up. I was supposed to ease her away quiet because you were making a play for her. He told me if you started anything I should smack you down quick."

Kent put in, "What happened when you recovered?"

"Mr. Firelli give me twenty bucks and said I wasn't tough enough for the joint."

I said, "That was certainly a dirty trick, Raoul."

He shrugged, drank the beer the waiter brought. "What the hell, twenty bucks is dough, and no manager to split it with."

I offered my hand. "Let's shake and forget it."

He grinned, relieved, and took the hand. He finished his beer and said he had to move on. Kent got up too.

He said, "I think I leave you in capable hands." He paused, frowned. "Did you say brown tweed?"

I had to do some agile mental back-tracking. "Yes. Raymond claimed the old man wore a blue serge or an Oxford gray in the afternoon, but sometimes changed at night."

Kent said, "I see," still puzzled. "Well, never mind. I won't need you this evening, but call between nine and ten anyway. And don't go to the hotel," he added over his shoulder. "I have my reputation to consider."

Jeannette watched him depart. "What'd he mean by that last crack?"

"Nothing. He's a great little kidder. What are you doing tonight?"

She thought about it, mollified. "Ain't it a little too early yet?"

A pair of arms went around my neck from behind, half in embrace, half stranglehold. A husky voice sang in my ear, "Hello, darling. They told me downtown you'd be here."

I broke the stranglehold, and turned to find the Gail fixing Jeannette with an ominous eye. I said feebly, "Hello, Bad News. Go away; I'm busy."

Jeannette said in a dangerous voice, "We're both busy. Pick yourself a different man."

The Gail smiled sweetly and dropped down beside me, practically in my lap. "I would, girlie, in a minute," she confided, "but he's the only husband I've got and I don't feel like going back to work."

Jeannette said sadly, "Oh, that's different." She sounded on the verge of tears.

I laughed in the manner of an embarrassed husband. "Well, honey, since you found me, how about a big kiss to show there's no hard feeling?"

I gave her a good squeeze to demonstrate what it felt like to be deprived of air. I kissed her noisily and simultaneously stepped on her toe. She kicked my shin deftly and tried to put out my eyes with her elbows. I released her in time to see Jeannette disappear into the mob at the bar. The Gail promptly moved over to the vacated seat.

"Buy me a drink, you lecherous pig," she demanded.

"Buy your own drinks." I gave her a nasty look. "Just because we happened to wake up together in the same bed once doesn't entitle you to haunt me. Last night you smacked my face and today I'm your loving husband."

She retorted, "You should thank me for saving you from that trollop."

I tried to stand up and suddenly discovered that my legs wouldn't hold me. I sat down again in a hurry.

The Gail crowed, pleased, "You can't leave. You're too drunk. Do you get drunk every night?"

"I'm on a rest cure—doctor's orders," I said, hurt. "Anyway, this is not drunkenness, merely temporary paralysis. Another drink will correct the condition."

"Or move it up to your head. What you need is food."

We compromised on two steaks while she made a valiant effort to catch up with me on drinks. By the time we finished eating we both felt well set up.

"Come on, let's go exploring," she coaxed.

"Nothing doing. I like it fine here. Did your pappy favor tweeds?"

She said promptly, "He never wore them. He claimed they were sloppy."

"That's funny."

"What's funny?"

"I don't know," I confessed. "I seem to have lost the thread of my thought."

"It'll come to you," she said practically. "It always does. Come on;

let's go places. My car is outside."

I refused obstinately. "No, you play too rough. I had all the bouncey I want last night and the night before. Kent asked me, as a personal favor, to keep out of trouble."

Fingers tapped on my shoulder. I looked up into a broad red face. It said, "Osmond wants to see you."

I shook my head. "Run along. I do not wish to see anybody." Two couples at a table a little way from our booth craned their necks and stopped talking.

A second voice said, "I'll give you a hand. He's soused again."

The Gail screamed, "Don't you dare touch him."

A badge flashed six inches from my nose. Red Face bent down. He said, "Listen, Phelps, they want you down at Headquarters. Nothing serious, just to answer a few questions. You don't want to make any trouble in a nice joint like this, do you?"

"I have to get my hat and coat," I stalled.

Red Face dangled them before me. I pulled myself erect and started to help the Gail get up. I was drunk, but knew that I could fight it off if I became angry enough. I said to the second dick who had shoved me aside and was pawing at the Gail, "Take your hands off her or I'll bend a chair over you thick skull."

He grated, "Why you—" and cuffed the side of my head. I tumbled in a heap, clutched at his legs as I fell and sank my teeth into his calf. He yelped in agony, tore himself free. He yanked a blackjack from his pocket and struck blindly down at me. I took the blow on my shoulder. The Gail sprang at his face. The place was in an uproar.

Red Face pulled her off, and grabbed his partner's arm before he could hit me again. He said, "Joe, are you crazy?"

"He bit me. The son of a gun bit me. Let me go. I'll kill him." His face bled from three long scratches.

I scrambled to my feet. I roared, "I'll chew his ear off next time."

Red Face had brawny arms hugging his partner's chest, pinning his hands at his sides. He said between gasps, "You and the dame go out to the car. The chauffeur will take you downtown. Don't try to get away, and for God's sake hurry. I can't hold him long."

Joe suddenly stopped struggling. He said in a normal voice, "I'm okay now. I swear I won't touch him."

Red Face relaxed his hold, but kept himself between us. He said, "You had no right to touch the dame. Come on."

We left. I was cold sober. The Gail walked without support but as though in a dream. Red Face kept pushing from behind, urging us out to the police car. He got in back with us. Joe climbed in with-the chauffeur. The car moved almost before he had slammed the door.

---

# CHAPTER 13

---

RED FACE spoke only once during the ride. He said under his breath, "You blasted fool. He mighta shot you."

I didn't answer. I wished I had taken Kent's advice about not gambling, about staying away from dizzy blondes and especially about keeping my nose out of the story. The Gail, huddled in a corner, clutched my hand as we slewed around a turn. Her fingernails dug into my palm. I was still wishing when we drew up before Police Headquarters.

Osmond, a wad of chewing tobacco bulging out his pock-marked cheek, squatted at an enormous desk facing the door. His china-blue eyes were half shut and practically hidden in folds of yellow fat. Two men sat at opposite corners of his desk. One was a police stenographer, the other District Attorney Hendrickson, who held a gold automatic pencil poised like a baton in his right hand.

Osmond boomed, "Well, well, Phelps. It was certainly decent of you to come." He shoved his paw at me.

I said, "Thanks. Now what is this all about?"

Osmond said cheerfully, "Just a few routine questions." Hendrickson nodded sage accord.

The questions were the same ones he had put the day before, except for their greater attention to detail. I did not say I had deliberately planned to get rid of Kent after dinner in order to meet the Gail, but I let them gather that impression. Hendrickson professed great surprise at my story of having been drugged, as though he were hearing it for the first time. He asked the Gail whether she could refresh my memory. She shook her head as though dazed.

Osmond said, "Now that's too bad." He sounded crestfallen. "If you could just kind of remember a little something—either one of you—we wouldn't need to trouble you no more."

I said, "I remember thinking it peculiar to find two law enforcement officials in a gambling house."

Hendrickson appealed to Osmond. "This fellow's arrogance is intolerable." He flung his pencil on the desk. Osmond's good humor vanished as though a spigot had been turned off. The muscles of his face bunched up, and little flecks danced in the china eyes.

"Listen, Phelps," he rumbled. His voice was like gathering thunder. "You're only making it tough for yourself. Maybe you're just dumb, so I'll ask you straight. Where's the papers Dillon was yelling about before he was croaked?" He held up a restraining hand. "I want you to think careful before you answer."

"I don't know. Why the devil should I know?"

Osmond said, "Don't be a jackass all your life. We're all pulling for the same thing. We got positive proof you were in the Dillon house during the night. You tell me where are them papers and I'll ease off the murder part. That's a promise."

I pretended to ponder. I said craftily, "How do you know I was there?"

He punched a button on his desk. A uniformed cop came in. "Bring up Collins," Osmond barked.

The cop left. The name Collins meant nothing to me. Osmond leaned back, chewing rhythmically. Hendrickson picked up his pencil and beat a nervous tattoo on the desk until Osmond, irritated, simply reached over and took the pencil out of his hands. The Gail's face looked like that of a person trying to wake from a nightmare.

The cop reappeared with a man in tow. Normally I might have taken him for a prosperous middle-aged business man. His clothes looked as though they had been made by a good tailor, even though they were badly mussed now. He had been terribly beaten. There was a lump under his right eye and his nose was a bloody mess. He walked carefully and with great effort.

Osmond waddled out from behind the desk. He shifted the cud from the left to his right cheek. He was wearing enormous green carpet slippers. He rolled over to Collins and pushed him playfully into a chair. Collins' head lolled.

Osmond said in his good-natured voice, "You recognize this guy, Miss Dillon?"

"I—yes." Her eyes clung to the mashed features in horrified fascination.

Hendrickson consulted his ever-present notes. "As I understand, you called on Mr. Dillon at one forty-five Monday night or, more accurately, Tuesday morning. Am I correct?"

The feeble twitch Hendrickson interpreted as assent. He supplied his own answer. "Correct. Your purpose, you would have us believe, in calling at so late an hour was to insure privacy."

For the first time Collins' eyes lost their death-house look. They became not hopeful, but alert and planning. He said, "The front door was open. Dillon always left it open for me, but this time there was no light in the foyer. While I hunted for the switch, I heard voices outside." He moistened his lips with a darting tongue. "I hid."

He pointed a long finger at the Gail, and she shrank back. I had a pretty clear idea of what was coming.

"She came in with a man. She was in front. I could see her face by the street light. She and the man went down the hall to the library."

Hendrickson interposed: "Had you previously entered the library?"

Collins shook his head vehemently. "They were right on top of me. I waited for them to get out of sight; then I slipped out. Honest to God, that's all I know."

Osmond started to rise, but Hendrickson restrained him. "Not quite all, Mr. Collins," he denied regretfully.

Collins stared about him blindly. He sobbed, "I can't stand any more. Yes, I waited in the little room until they came down. She was carrying a bag. Then I went into the library and found Dillon on the floor."

Hendrickson nodded encouragement.

"All I took was the picture—I swear. I never even heard of any papers. Dillon owed me money—that's what I called about. He was paying me off a little at a time. The picture was a photo showing the two of us at the speakers' table of a banquet given by my firm, Midwest Smelting and Refining. I'm one of the directors. It isn't as big a job as it sounds, but I do have charge of some investments. Dillon persuaded me to speculate with the firm's money. When we were wiped out he offered to make good the loss if I kept quiet about it."

"How much was involved?"

"Eleven thousand dollars. He had already repaid four thousand. When I saw he was dead I lost my head. I cut the picture from its frame because I was afraid it might lead a trail back to me. I thought if the police found out about the money they might think I had murdered Jeffrey."

Hendrickson purred, "You positively identify Miss Dillon as the woman you saw?"

"Yes. Before we had the trouble over the money I visited Mr. Dillon's house several times and met his family."

Osmond said, "And this other feller—I mean the feller with her —did you get a good look at him?"

Collins searched my face. He said hesitantly, "I'm not sure. He had his coat collar turned up."

Osmond muttered under his breath and punched the call button. William, the cop, came in so fast he must have been waiting in an adjoining room.

Collins' eyes rolled with fear. "I recognize him now. I wasn't sure at first."

Osmond sneered, "By God, then stay sure." He motioned to the cop. "Take this guy back downstairs and have him cleaned up. Let a doctor look at his nose. And lay off the rough stuff. First thing you know, the department will be getting a bad name."

William snickered as at a joke. He took Collins by the arm and led him out. Osmond and Hendrickson sat back, waiting. I thought, Here it comes. Confused memories jostled inside my head, but when I tried to grasp them they eluded me.

Osmond's voice recalled me. He pronounced, "Chester Phelps, I charge you with the murder of Jeffrey Dillon."

I couldn't believe my ears. "Wait a minute. You don't take that goofy story seriously. He simply said what he thought you wanted to hear."

Osmond said, "You had your chance."

Hendrickson said formally, "We shall be glad to take any statement you wish to make with the express understanding that you are promised nothing."

I took a deep breath. "A couple of hours from now, when your butchers finish working me over, you'll ask whether I'm willing to trade a confession for a night's sleep. All right. You can lock me up and maybe even beat a confession out of me, but when Kent finishes with you two and the crooked crowd you front for, there won't be enough left to scrape up with a spoon."

Osmond knocked over his chair in his haste to get at me. I hunched my shoulders and waited for his rush. The Gail sprang to her feet, blocking him. She cried, "Oh please, don't. I'll tell you what you want to know."

Osmond stopped abruptly, turned back to his desk. He picked up his chair and lowered his enormous bulk. Benevolence spread all over his face.

The Gail stared past me. She said, "I'll tell, but not while Chet is here. Please send him out."

Hendrickson said with unction, "Why, certainly, Miss Dillon."

Osmond punched the bell, and after a while the cop came in. "Take this guy outside and wait," Osmond instructed.

William walked over to me. He said in a menacing voice, "Come on, bub."

I saw no point in anticipating the pounding bound to come. I let him march me through a rear door into a small anteroom that had only one window with a grill over it. It had only a bench against the wall and a desk and chair for furniture. I sat down on the bench. William displayed a revolver, which he placed on the desk. He stated his position. "Don't start nothing, and I won't."

It was almost an hour later before the buzzer on the desk sounded. William went outside, after carefully locking the corridor door. He was back in a moment. "They want you." He stepped aside to let me pass.

Osmond and Hendrickson were still behind the big desk, but the stenographer had left. The Gail sat in the chair Collins had occupied. Hendrickson shuffled his notes. The Gail kept her face immobile.

Osmond invited, "Sit down."

I sat down. My knees suddenly felt weak.

Osmond added, "We all make these mistakes, sonny. Now you were kind of rough on Joe back there." He looked serious. "Assaulting an officer ain't no joke." He had an inspiration. "By God, I'll tell you what I'll do. You overlook what happened and I'll see Joe don't press no charges."

I picked up my hat and said to the Gail, "Coming?"

She rose quickly, stepped beside me. I said to Osmond, "Speaking as a reporter, what disposition is being made of Collins? Or does he also rate one of your handsome hand-engraved apologies?"

Osmond said, "What a kidder. You and me could be real good friends, by God." He crossed his paws over his belly. "Collins has been charged with murder. He'll be arraigned in the morning. That's official."

"Are you sure it's okay with Firelli?"

Nothing could jolt Osmond out of his placidity. He said amiably, "For a young feller you got the nastiest disposition I ever seen. It'll land you in trouble some day, damned if it won't."

I didn't think up an answer to that one until we were outside. I looked up and down for a cab, said to the Gail, "Goodbye, now," and walked rapidly toward the corner.

Her heels beat a quick tattoo as she almost ran to keep up with me. I stopped. I said patiently, "Look lady, this is the end of the line —the last stop. You see before you a man who knows when he is licked. I stuck my head into a noose for you, up there. It was a very uncomfortable sensation. I do not wish another taste of it. So run along and do not bother the animals further."

She said, "I'm not following you. Besides, don't you want to know what I told them?"

"Positively not. I'm through with curiosity forever. Let the Kents of the world solve its murders. They have the knack. The diet is too rich for my blood. Why don't you go home?"

"Collins didn't murder my father. Thomas Morgan did. I saw him."

I groaned. A cruising cab turned the corner and slowed down as the driver spotted us. I grabbed the Gail's wrist. I said, "If this is a gag, I'll choke you with my bare hands, so help me."

She said, "I saw him. I swear I did."

I hailed the cab. I said, "Hold your hats, boys; here we go again."

# CHAPTER 14

KENT looked up crossly as we entered. He said, "When I ask you to phone me at a specified hour, I expect—" He bit the words off, and his eyes hardened, as he caught sight of the Gail half hidden behind me.

The Gail returned his glare with interest. She said furiously, "If that's the way you feel, I'm sorry I came." She made for the door.

I said, "Wait a minute—both of you." I closed the door, put my back against it. "Miss Dillon's here to tell us all about the murder of her pappy, which same she now recalls having witnessed."

She blazed, "I never said I saw him killed." She gave me a stormy look. "Chet made that part up." Her lower lip trembled. "But I know just the same," she added lamely. "Thomas Morgan killed my father."

"Wait a minute," I objected. I faced the Gail. "Outside the police station you told me you saw Morgan kill your father. Now you give us the business of female intuition. What is this—some kind of a game you play?"

She faltered, "I—I'm sorry. When I left the house at nine-thirty I didn't drive into the country. I went to the Club Cabana. But I didn't go in. I sat in my car for a few minutes, then decided I had made a mistake in leaving my father alone. I turned around and hurried back home."

"How long did it take you to return?"

"About fifteen minutes."

Kent nodded.

"As I turned into our street I saw a man go up the front stairs of our house. By the time my car drew up he was already inside. I parked down the block and waited for perhaps ten minutes, but he didn't come out. It occurred to me then how foolishly I was behaving. I drove back to the Club Cabana and arrived there at a quarter of eleven, as I told the police."

"And your contention is that the man you saw was Mr. Morgan?"

"His back was turned to me, but I recall instantly thinking it was Mr. Morgan, so I must have recognized something about him—his build or the way he walked."

Kent sucked in his breath, exasperated. "You were piloting a moving vehicle on a dark street. Identification under those conditions is well nigh impossible."

"There is a street lamp almost in front of our door."

He shook his head emphatically. "Let it pass for the moment. Are there further variations from your original story?"

"No. I phoned Daddy from the club just as I said."

"And you wish to add nothing concerning events later in the night?"

"No."

"You are mistaken," Kent said with icy calm. "You have a great deal to add. As, for example, the reason why Mr. Firelli paid one Raoul Langueste twenty dollars to stage a fight with Chet. And why Chet was drugged."

Her cheeks flamed. "I wanted to meet Chet, and Firelli said he would arrange it. I didn't realize he would pick such a horrible way." Her fingers worked convulsively. "And I didn't know Chet was drugged. He merely seemed very drunk. I always thought people became unconscious when they were drugged."

"Not invariably. I have been—ah—reading on the subject. The actions of drugs differ considerably. Please continue."

"After we cashed in, Chet suggested we try another gambling house, but I knew we'd simply lose all our winnings. Besides, I was anxious to go home but afraid to do so alone. Instead of sobering up, Chet fell asleep. I didn't dare go home then. Instead, I took Chet to my apartment."

Kent said, "In short, you ask me to put no credence whatever in the story wrung from Mr. Collins simply because you managed, in some fashion, to secure Chet's and your own release from custody. You claim to have gone directly to your apartment in the company of a sodden stranger merely because you feared to return home

alone." Annoyance flitted across his face. "Really, it outrages me
to be considered so credulous. No, indeed, you took Chet home as
planned and, upon entering the library, found your father's body.
Realizing immediately your lack of an alibi for the probable time of
the murder, you manufactured what you hoped would be one."

The droop of her shoulders was confirmation enough.

"You went upstairs, packed a bag, even provided pajamas, a shirt
and tie for Chet, to make the rendezvous appear prearranged, and
proceeded to your apartment. Naturally, you had no means of knowing you had been observed by Mr. Collins."

She said nothing. After a moment Kent shrugged and said, "Miss
Dillon, you mix truth and falsehood indiscriminately and with disas-
trous results. For example, you say you left your home at nine-thirty,
drove to the Cabana—a matter of fifteen minutes or so—then returned in time to see Mr. Morgan arrive. This would put you back
before your house shortly aften ten. By your own account, again,
you returned to the Cabana after vainly waiting ten minutes for Mr.
Morgan to emerge. Still accepting your own time schedule, you arrived at the Cabana not later than twenty minutes past ten and
waited forty minutes before calling your father."

The Gail flashed, "What's impossible about that?"

"Nothing," he assured her. "Nothing at all. But Mr. Morgan, who,
by the way, admits his visit to the house, places himself there shortly
before ten-thirty, thus creating an all-important differential of at
least twenty minutes between your version and his."

"I have nothing more to say."

He sat erect. "I suggest that the certainty of your identification
lies in a slight distortion of the facts. You did indeed see Mr. Morgan, but not under the circumstances you described. You were inside,
not your car, but the house. You had already discovered your father's
body, or, if not, you had just arrived and hid when you heard footsteps in the hall. You observed Mr. Morgan much as Mr. Collins later
spied on you."

She cried, "No, no."

Kent held up a restraining hand. "Please—no more lies. Were
you inside the house or were you not?"

"I was inside." Her voice sank to an intense whisper. "But my
father's body was not there. You must believe me."

"And you spoke to him subsequently?"

"Yes."

"Can you not be mistaken?"

"I know my father's voice." They were the same words she had said to me.

Kent shook his head in frank bewilderment. "I have no choice but to believe you. At what time were you in the house?"

"Just before ten-thirty."

"And where did you spend the intervening time?"

She said stubbornly, "I won't tell. I can't."

"Very well. I think I can guess, but I shall not trouble at the moment. Did Mr. Morgan enter the house?"

"Just as far as the foyer."

"And you left immediately thereafter, returning to the Cabana, which you reached shortly before eleven. Am I correct?"

"Yes."

Kent said, "Thank you. I shall not tax your amiability with further questions, since we are now in a position to make at least a partial reconstruction of last Monday night's events." He stood up, walked around to the front of his desk and leaned against it.

"Let us establish the background of the crime. Jeffrey Dillon is alone in his house—at the very outset a false note. A man in constant fear of his life avoids solitude, seeks rather to surround himself with family and retainers. Only highly cogent reasons would prompt him to risk an evening of solitude. Thus far, no such reason has been discovered."

"Maybe he meant to leave and changed his mind," the Gail offered timidly.

"A man who fears for his life does not easily change his mind."

I said, "Collins. If his story is true, he had a late appointment with Dillon, who had roped him on a bum investment. He was probably threatening Dillon with exposure."

"There was no reason for them to transact their business in the dead of night like a pair of conspirators."

I shrugged. "All right, I give up. We haven't found the how-come of his consuming yen for privacy. But that doesn't prove he had no reason."

"True enough. Except for modifying circumstances, we might be compelled to seek it further. The first of these is Mr. Dillon's call to his partner, substantiated beyond doubt. If he intended to keep the appointment, his privacy was automatically limited to about two hours, allowing thirty minutes for the trip to Morgan's apartment. Note, in passing, that the appointment with Morgan destroys the likelihood of one with Collins.

"Consider, however, the psychological effect of the conversation with Morgan. The spectre of incriminating papers is raised. Is this the course of a man who seeks to insure privacy for the sake of which he presumably risks his life? I think not."

I said, "What you mean is that Dillon was trying to make sure he wouldn't have privacy."

"Precisely. The spectacle of a man who fears for his safety, yet deliberately courts attack—who threatens dangerous associates with exposure and then clears the way for his enemies by invitingly remaining in a deserted house—all this is a study in paradox. Your father's intent was an ancient device served up in modern fashion. Mr. Dillon intended merely to vanish."

The Gail threw back her head and laughed. It didn't sound funny to me.

Kent remarked, "You evidently agree, Chet."

I nodded. "It's a natural."

He beamed. "As you say—a natural. It explains the need for a brief period of privacy, the lure of an appointment with Morgan which, when not kept, might be counted upon to bring Morgan or Firelli to the house."

The Gail said, "You're both crazy."

"No. We are not crazy," Kent said with certainty. "The apartment rented by Clarice Dill—was it not for the purpose of providing your father with a convenient hideout?"

"No."

"Please." Kent gestured irritably. "Do not take me for a child. You are a very foolish young woman in some respects, but not the sort to maintain a *boite*. Only an ass like Osmond or a lecher like Hendrickson would lend credence to so absurd a fiction."

She said faintly, "I suppose I should thank you."

"Rubbish." He looked uncomfortable. "Where—ah—was I? Oh, yes. The pajamas Chet wore, the shirt and tie. All these brand-new, and purchased in advance by Mr. Dillon against the moment of his flight. No wonder Hendrickson attached no importance to the pajamas, since they were not remotely similar to those affected by your late father. And the strangely initialed hat—all these fit into the patterns of a newly created personality."

"Don't forget the brown tweeds he 'never' wore," I prompted. A sudden thought struck me. I said sadly, "It's no good. We've forgotten those blasted phone calls. If Dillon expected to skip, he wouldn't return at eleven. He'd be smart enough to figure either Morgan or Firelli might decide to jump the appointment."

Kent looked at the Gail. "How about it, Miss Dillon?"

She shrugged. "Why bother asking me? You won't believe my

answer."

Kent inclined his head. "I have already told you I do believe you. I must, though for reasons entirely apart from what you say. Let us put it that for an undisclosed purpose Mr. Dillon left his home as planned, then returned only to be caught and killed."

I said, "All right, let's get on with it. Dillon set the stage for a disappearance that was to smell of murder. But somebody came along and supplied the one missing detail—Dillon's body. The rest should be a cinch. Who done it?"

Kent said, "Ungrammatical but forceful. Who indeed? If you will answer two preliminary questions I shall be delighted to name the murderer."

"Fire away," I invited.

"Why was the body mutilated and why were the false faces painted?"

I smiled at the Gail, who gave me back an unwinking stare. I said, "You mean we really don't know a damn thing."

"On the contrary. We know a great deal, even though much of it is negative. We have had mixed in a single box the parts of two distinct picture puzzles. We have now separated our puzzles and eliminated one set of pieces—those having to do with Jeffrey Dillon's planned disappearance and pseudo-murder. Except as they may provide a clue to his actual death, we can ignore the missing papers, Mr. Dillon's loudly voiced fears, blackmail and the paradox of privacy that was not private. You see, we have made considerable progress, even though it be of a destructive nature. On the positive side, we must now seek a motive powerful enough to make Mr. Dillon desire to vanish."

"To hell with this talky-talk," I erupted. "All I see is that Dillon didn't have the faintest notion of the direction his death was coming from. Never mind why he wanted to skip. Who could know about it? Not Morgan—or Firelli—or Collins."

I looked at the Gail, who turned white.

I said, "You—you knew. You provided the hideout. You were the one member of the family he trusted. Yours is the only alibi not worth a penny. You sold him out. Of course he was there at eleven—with a gun in his back—kept alive long enough for you and your accomplice to cook up an alibi for later—for the time when you knew in advance he would be dead."

The Gail leaped to her feet. Kent said sharply, "Sit down." She sank back in her chair, looking at me as though I were something loathsome.

The private phone rang. Kent ordered irritably, "For goodness sake answer it."

It was Cafferty breathlessly demanding Kent. I switched on the extension, and listened in as Kent picked up his receiver.

Kent said, "Go ahead, Cafferty."

Cafferty said, "That punk, Jack Lugoni, you wanted a line on, Mr. Kent. He's dead. We just got the report at Police Headquarters. He was riding in a Cadillac with two unidentified men about a half-hour ago. They slowed down for a light to change at Main and Ninth when another car drew alongside and fired two shotgun bursts into them. The Caddy crashed, but the driver and another man got away before the squad cars arrived. The ambulance surgeon listed Lugoni as dead on arrival."

"What else?"

"The word is going around that Firelli killed his own man because Lugoni went over to the downstate mob. It looks like a full-fledged gang war is ready to bust loose."

"Nice work, Cafferty," Kent approved. "Hold on while I switch you to rewrite. Keep in touch with Jake. If Firelli is arrested, call me personally; otherwise make further reports to the Desk. Jake will send out as many more men as necessary to cover the situation."

He dropped the receiver, and I shifted the call to Jake. Kent said to me, "Apparently your friends persuaded Mr. Lugoni to throw in his lot with them. It appears to have been an unwise decision."

I groaned. "I don't feel well. I think I feel a case of lead poisoning coming on."

He put his fingertips together and regarded me over them. "How does it feel to be a freelance master mind at this moment?"

I didn't answer.

Kent regarded the Gail thoughtfully, picked up his phone. "Is Miss Benton in? Good. I should like to see her at once."

The Gail said, "Please, I think I'll go home, after all."

Kent shook his head. "We cannot afford to let anything happen to you, Miss Dillon."

I gasped. "You mean she's in actual danger?"

"I mean nothing," he snapped. "Neither can I see any advantage in running unnecessary risks. Miss Dillon is in some fashion mixed up with Firelli, who is at the moment running amok."

The Gail's tragic face was more eloquent than words.

"Miss Benton will take you to a hotel. Do not register under your own name. You are not to leave your room for any reason until you hear further from me."

He had her thoroughly scared now. She said, "I understand."

Kent picked up the phone and asked for Jake. He drummed on the desk top while the connection was being made. "Jake? Dig out everything incriminating against Commissioner Osmond. Don't go back more than a year. Announce a series of articles revealing the tie-up between high administration officials and the criminal elements of our city. Suggest the possibility that Jack Lugoni, killed tonight, was murdered because he shifted his allegiance from Firelli to the invading gangsters. What? I can't help that. Our hand has been forced. If we are threatened, call the Burns Agency for six of their best operatives to protect the Free Press building." He hung up.

The phone rang again. The night operator on the switchboard said, "Say, Chet, there's a dame on the wire says she's gotta talk to Kent very private."

"Who is she?"

"She won't give her name."

"What is all this palaver?" Kent fumed.

"A lady who wants to talk to you very private, won't give her name," I reported.

"Well, put her on, for heaven's sake."

I didn't point out that he never accepted phone calls without first learning the identity of the caller, simply gave the operator the order to put the lady through and prepared to listen.

Antoine's hoarse voice came over the wire. "Is this Kent?"

"Yes."

She evidently didn't intend to waste time over preliminaries. "I've decided to take you up on that offer for my life story, Kent. You can have it for five thousand dollars."

Kent smiled into the mouthpiece. "A few hours ago you tried to kill Mr. Morgan and my secretary, Phelps. Aren't you afraid we'll have your call traced and turn you over to the police?"

The gasp from behind me was the Gail. I turned to face her and saw that she was staring at me with horror. I winked and held my forefinger against my heart, cocked my thumb for a trigger and pressed it. The Gail gave a satisfying little scream. Kent glared at me, but I pretended not to catch his signal.

Antoine said, "Nuts, I fired over that goofy reporter's head. I wouldn't even have done that if the dope hadn't tried to tackle me. All I wanted was to scare Morgan into keeping away from his wife."

Kent said, "You missed Chet, perhaps deliberately, but you shot Mr. Morgan."

There was a moment's silence. Then she said calmly, "You're a liar. I read all the papers and there wasn't anything about it."

"At Mr. Morgan's own request, but you shot him just the same."

"All right," she said truculently. "So I shot him. What the hell of it? He won't prosecute."

"You sound very sure of yourself."

She said, "Listen, I haven't got all night. Do you want to buy my story or not?"

"Will it include the name of Mr. Dillon's murderer?"

"Yes."

Miss Benton came in. She was a large, capable maiden with the face of a sympathetic horse, and could get stories under conditions that would stymie the best man on the staff. I reluctantly put down the extension phone and gave Benton instructions concerning the Gail. Benton got it immediately and took the Gail into her custody. The Gail left without a word to me. I grabbed up the extension again.

Antoine was saying, "At my apartment. Bring the money with you, nothing bigger than a twenty, and not before one or one-thirty. I've got a few loose ends to tidy up first."

"Isn't that a rather late hour to come calling?" Kent objected.

"You can take it or leave it."

"Very well, at one-thirty," he conceded.

"I'll tell the elevator operator I'm expecting a late visitor, so you won't have any trouble getting up. Don't forget what I said about the money."

"I won't," he promised, and hung up.

# CHAPTER 15

I TOOK a bite of the ham sandwich and washed it down with a slug of lukewarm coffee. At my elbow was a bottle labeled "Scotch-Type Scotch." It tasted like embalming fluid. We were back to normal.

Kent checked the last sheet of copy on the St. Arles life story as dreamed up by a pair of overworked reporters. It was a nicely balanced concoction, half Elsie Dinsmore, half Snappy Stories, and all flung together from morgue clippings running back to the days when Antoine had enjoyed minor fame as a night-club singer. All the story needed was the name of Dillon's murderer to transform it from a lifeless rewrite of stale news paragraphs into a sizeable chunk of dynamite.

I finished the coffee, lit a cigarette. I inquired idly, "What do we get for our money, apart from fifteen thousand words of tripe?"

Kent flipped the pages. "We shall have Miss St. Arles' by-line. At the moment she is a figure of national interest."

"Who you kidding?" I scoffed. "The Free Press never went for stuff like that. I'll bet she intends to use the story as a lever to work some high-class blackmail in the right quarters. And if we print any guesses or opinions about the identity of the murderer, we'll be up to our ears in libel suits and in a jam with the D.A."

Kent said gravely, "Miss St. Arles' by-line is worth five thousand dollars, if not to the Free Press, then to the Allied Syndicate. If she chooses to accuse some person, she does so on her own responsibility and at her own peril. As for libel, I anticipate a solution to the crime long before we get to the point of naming names."

I said, "Oh, oh, light dawns. You think publishing an installment of this mess will bring the killer out into the open with a move against St. Arles. I know she tried to shoot me, but isn't that a low trick to play on her?"

Kent said, still gravely, "Miss St. Arles must know the implications of a published story. Whether or not her life is endangered depends entirely upon her subsequent actions. My own belief is that she intends to go into hiding for a time."

I yawned. "Well, this is one hunk of blood that won't be on my head."

Kent put on his hat and coat. I said, doing likewise, "I don't like anything about this set-up. Suppose we walk into some kind of a trap."

Kent said sharply, "I have taken that possibility into consideration. You are not to come with me. If I don't return or call you within an hour, take whatever measures you deem advisable."

I snorted. "If we're going, skip the heroics and let's be on our way. You're not going alone even if I have to knock you down and sit on your chest."

He glared at me, and I glared right back. Then he smiled, and I felt foolish as I trailed him outside. We got a break when we found Mickey's cab parked in the street.

Kent said, "The Albermarle Apartments."

The cab jolted to life and raced through the deserted streets at a speed surprising for its age.

At the Albermarle Kent gave Mickey specific instructions about what to do in case we failed to come down reasonably soon. We went inside. The night elevator operator said, "Miss St. Arles phoned down that she was expecting a Mr. Kent. That your name?"

Kent admitted his identity, and we rode to the fourth floor. I led the way to Apartment G and pushed the bell button. The elevator door closed and the car started back down. There was no answer to my ring.

I said, "I don't like this. Call the elevator back."

"Nonsense. Try it again." He rattled the doorknob. The door swung open at his touch. The foyer was in semi-darkness, faintly lighted from a table lamp within the room. No sound reached us.

I said more urgently, "Let's get out of here. I smell trouble."

Kent said, "It's too late now." He stepped over the threshold. "Come in and close the door."

She was in the bedroom, stretched out on the floor. A puddle of blood spread fanwise from the body. There were half a dozen of the grinning false faces on the bedroom walls, drawn with what looked like lipstick. No false face had been painted on the body. As I took in the sight I could feel a pulse throbbing in my forehead. Kent stood in the open doorway.

I said, "The false faces—all over again."

Kent said very quietly, "Yes, but with a difference. There are fewer of them, the body is not mutilated, and her own face has not been masked."

"No. We've got to beat it. We can be analytical later."

I hustled him out of the bedroom, wiping the door handle with my handkerchief again. I told him to ring for the elevator and started to wipe the outside door handle, but remembered not to just in time. I left the door slightly ajar.

When I heard the elevator door open I groused, "I'm sorry you feel that way, Miss St. Arles. We offered you a good proposition. If you think you can do better elsewhere, go ahead and try." I slammed the door and followed Kent into the elevator. The operator looked at us sleepily.

At any second I expected to hear the scream of sirens. I was afraid Kent would say something unnatural, but he had sense enough to keep quiet. We reached the sidewalk.

I shoved him ahead of me into the cab and told Mickey to drive around the corner. I said, "I haven't the time to argue with you now. Go back to the office and stay there. If the cops arrive before I do, say you sent me out on a hot lead. Stall them as long as you can."

I hopped out of the cab before he could answer, waved Mickey away. I ducked into the shadows and spent a few precious seconds cursing Kent for putting us into such a predicament.

Keeping to the shadows, I went down the service entrance of the Albermarle. I found an unlocked door to the furnace room, and there a stairway that led to the rear of the lobby. I went up cautiously. The elevator operator dozed in a chair before the switchboard. I went up behind him, put my right hand over his mouth, and caught his neck in the crook of my left arm. He made incoherent noises.

I lowered my voice to a bass croak. "What floor does the St. Arlès dame live on?" I grated. I relaxed the hand over his mouth.

He gasped, "Fourth floor, Apartment G."

"Is this on the level?"

He babbled something about taking me up. I cackled hideously in his ear and yanked him out of the chair. I flipped him around, concealed my face behind one shoulder and dealt him a quick, merciful blow on the point of his chin. He swooned, as much from terror as from the wallop. When he came to I knew he would give a graphic description of the six or seven armed thugs who had overpowered him.

I dumped him in the elevator and ran it to the basement. I couldn't find any rope, but did stumble over a pile of soiled towels and used a few of these to tie him up clumsily. I rolled him out on the ground, then ran the elevator to the fourth floor.

In Antoine's apartment I risked a minute or two over the corpse without learning anything new. I found Antoine's purse. It contained about eighty dollars in cash. There were no letters or papers. Neither the bedroom nor the living room had been searched.

Plagiarizing Jeffrey Dillon, I tossed the bedroom around to give the appearance of a terrific struggle. I was careful to wipe anything I had touched and, this time, included the front doorknob, now that the presence of an intruder had been established.

I ran the elevator back to the basement and had negotiated the passageway to the service entrance before I heard the shrill whine of the sirens, still a little way off. I walked rapidly down the block, keeping to the shadows as much as possible. When I reached Willis Street, two blocks from the Albermarle, I steered an erratic course toward an all-night cab stand and practically fell into the arms of a taxi driver.

We held a brief drunken debate, and then I let him drive me to Union Terminal, where I paid without protest a fare approximately four times what it should have been, thus insuring that my driver would forever after deny having met me.

In the station I bought three magazines and rolled them into a tight ball. I sat for over an hour in the men's smoking room and pretended to be asleep. At the end of that time a train arrived, and I mingled with the departing sleepy passengers, all similarly equipped with soiled magazines.

I took a cab from the station to within two blocks of the Free Press building and walked the rest of the way, satisfied I had covered my tracks as carefully as possible.

## CHAPTER 16

I FOUND Kent knee-deep in lawyers. He was sitting back in his chair, half asleep, a bored expression on his face. A couple of lawyers were at my desk hanging on the phone. Three others had their heads together over in one corner. Silver-haired old Arthur Campbell, himself, who wouldn't leave his office for anybody on earth except Kent, had this time apparently left his bed as well and was stalking up and down the room, issuing orders, waving his arms and raving.

When he saw me, Kent said in his most surly manner, "It's high time you showed up. I can't be expected to hold off single-handed the entire armed forces of a city."

Arthur Campbell stopped marching and confronted me. "Was this your idea? Do you realize Mr. Kent has laid himself open to the most serious consequences?"

"I don't know what goes on," I protested. "I merely told Kent to stall if the cops came here before I did."

Kent shouted, "The scoundrel actually has the temerity to demand my presence in his filthy station house."

I said, "Ah ha, you're afraid. What do you think they'll do—beat you with a rubber hose?"

Kent muttered darkly but did not meet my eye. Campbell started swearing again. He said, "Judge Callahan is willing to issue a writ of habeas corpus the moment Mr. Kent is taken into custody. He's been waiting since two-thirty." He churned his arms. "How the brass-bound hell can I demand a writ for a man who isn't arrested yet?" He appealed to me.

I said reproachfully, "I'm ashamed of you, Mr. Kent. Why, you're nothing but a 'fraidy cat."

Kent smacked his palm on the desktop. He roared, "Freedom of the press," stalked into the study and banged the door behind him with an air of finality.

I asked, "Is there a warrant out for either of us?"

Campbell pointed sweepingly to his battery of lawyers. "Osmond hasn't found a judge yet who dares to issue one, but he will pretty soon. He's bound to. Kent can't get away with this indefinitely."

The phone on Kent's desk rang. I picked it up. It was Kent, from the inner room. He said, "Get rid of those people. I want to sleep."

I said to Arthur, "Mr. Kent wants to sleep."

Arthur snatched his coat. "For all of me he can rot in jail the rest of his life. I'm through."

When they had gone I picked up the phone and asked the operator to locate the district attorney. After a considerable wait I reached him.

I said, "Hello, Mr. District Attorney, this is Phelps."

Hendrickson said frigidly, "I thought Kent was calling."

"He'd like to, but the trouble is he's dangerously sick." I made my voice confidential. "He has a bad heart, you know. When he learned about Miss St. Arles being killed only a few minutes after he had seen her, it almost finished him."

Hendrickson yelped with indignation and spluttered that Kent could have his doctor with him when he appeared for questioning.

I said as though relieved, "Fine, but I still don't feel you should be made to wait several days until Mr. Kent is able to get about. After all, murder has been done, and time is important."

Hendrickson said, "Ah—please be more concrete."

"Gladly. Miss St. Arles phoned us last night with an offer of exclusive rights to her life story, including the name of Jeffrey Dillon's murderer. In the interests of justice Mr. Kent and I hastened to her apartment only to find her demands preposterous— twenty thousand dollars instead of the five she had originally demanded. Mr. Kent refused to accept such terms and we left."

"Interesting if true. Why didn't Kent come to me with this story?"

"I just told you why. He's a very very sick man. Now here is my suggestion. As proof of our changed attitude, we'll withdraw from later editions today the article attacking Commissioner Osmond and print a retraction."

Hendrickson said, "Well, I'll call you back."

When he called back a few minutes later his voice was warm and gracious. "I have good news for you, Phelps. Your account of what happened at the Albemarle has just been confirmed reliably from another source. Please tell Mr. Kent that we will positively not have to trouble him further."

We went through a little act in which I said Kent insisted on appearing and Hendrickson as firmly declined. I said, "How did the police happen to find the body so soon?"

"Through an anonymous phone call."

"Was the name of the murderer mentioned?"

Hendrickson said, "Well—no. Not exactly."

I said, "You sound as though you have some kind of a lead. Give us a break on the story, Mr. Hendrickson."

He said as though reaching a quick decision. "I will. Our office is convinced that Firelli is at the bottom of these crimes."

I said, "Tsk, tsk."

Hendrickson warmed to his subject. He said indignantly, "I had no idea of his villainous character. You know, of course, that he shot a man in cold blood yesterday. And this morning, when a police officer was sent to pick him up, Firelli almost killed him also."

"May we print that?"

"You certainly may. Sergeant O'Connor is at Mercy Hospital. He was shot in the thigh while bravely trying to apprehend a vicious killer—Firelli. You may further say that all exits from the city are being watched. Firelli will be shot on sight." His voice quivered with righteous anger.

I thanked him profusely, and we parted with many protestations of mutual esteem.

I phoned outside to Jake and told him the war was over.

He said mournfully, "Don't tell me the ornery son of a gun is getting away with it."

"I'm afraid so," I admitted. "Kill the article about Osmond and crime in our fair city, also the gang war stuff. Announce that it was all a vicious rumor." I told him the latest about Firelli. "I guess Osmond and Hendrickson decided Firelli was getting too hot for them. Kent is snoozing in the study. I'll catch up on a little shut-eye myself. If anything special breaks, wake Kent but don't bother me."

I went into the study. Kent was really asleep. With supreme confidence he had undressed completely. I lay down on the other bed, fully clothed and dog-tired. Kent's tranquil snores filled the room. . . .

I wakened to find Cafferty shaking me. He said, "You sure are a deep sleeper."

I said, "Go away. What time is it?"

"A quarter to eleven. Kent wants you."

"Tell him to pick on somebody else. The cops are all squared."

"Raymond Dillon is outside," Cafferty persisted. "His Nibs wants you to sit in on the powwow."

Kent and Raymond were alone in the office when I entered. Raymond had been speaking, but fell silent when he saw me. I sat down at my desk.

Kent said, "Please continue, Mr. Dillon."

"I have no more to say. If you will tell me where my sister is, I will leave at once."

"When did you see your sister last?"

"Yesterday afternoon, shortly after Phelps left the house. She went out without saying where. I assumed she intended to meet him."

Kent said, "I see." I caught his eye, and he shook his head slightly. He studied his fingernails and Raymond smoked. Finally Kent said, "Frankly, I don't know your sister's whereabouts. However, I imagine you will hear from her later in the day."

Raymond appeared relieved. He said, "I understand," which was more than I did.

"Can you account for your own time last night?" Kent inquired.

"Of course. I spent the evening at Miss Todd's home. Afterwards I went to the University Club. I arrived home about one or a trifle earlier. This morning I was told my sister's bed had not been slept in. The police came a little while later. They asked for Gail. I told them she had gone out very early, and came here as soon as they finished questioning us."

"Very sensible. I suggest you go about your business and say nothing. Your sister is bound to learn of the murder and realize the necessity of communicating with you. If she does not turn up by mid-afternoon, there will still be time to consider other measures."

Raymond asked abruptly, "Do you believe the murder of my father grew out of the revelations made in those articles about him last year?"

Kent shot him a keen glance. "The possibility is remote."

"Where did you get the information for the articles?" Raymond persisted.

"I cannot divulge our sources, but your father was not one of them."

Raymond said, "Be frank, Mr. Kent, and admit you don't know where your leads came from."

Kent said slowly, "I suspected a member of the family, but Mrs. Dillon rather than you." He looked at the boy with renewed interest.

Raymond said defiantly, "Mother wasn't involved. Every bit of it came from me. I suppose you're thinking what a filthy thing it was to do."

"Really, you surprise me," Kent stated. "I least of all would be likely to censure you. Whatever your motive, you rendered a great service to your city."

Raymond said soberly, "I sent you that stuff to strike back at my father because I had been goaded beyond endurance. I think now he followed a deliberate course, as though he actually wanted to be betrayed."

Kent glanced at me, and I nodded.

"I'm not a clever person," Raymond continued. "I'm not even a good liar." He smiled faintly. "I mentioned being at the University Club last night. The truth is I had been living there for the past three months and until a little more than a week ago."

"You returned home at your father's request?"

"Yes. I wish I could make you understand the sort of man he was. He delighted in torturing people. He despised me, but it didn't suit his whim to have me far out of reach. About two years ago Gail and I were left a small inheritance. Since then I have been less dependent on him." He paused as though to collect his thoughts. "He went out of his way to show me the workings of his underworld connections. He literally dared me to expose him."

"Did your father object to your marrying Miss Todd?"

Raymond met his gaze squarely. "He didn't care for her at first, then changed his mind as he grew to know her better. As a matter of fact, I would not have returned home this last time had not my fiancée urged the reconciliation."

Kent nodded. He said casually, "Just one thing more, Mr. Dillon. Why did you impersonate your father's voice?"

The boy sat silent. Presently he said, "I suppose that means you think I killed my father."

"I think nothing."

The phone rang. It was Katie to tell me that Laura Todd was outside. Kent instructed, "Have her come in."

No more was said until she arrived. She threw a searching glance at Kent. Raymond stood up. Laura went to him and took his hand. She said, "Have you told them?"

He said in a low voice, "No."

"Please, Raymond, I think you should."

Kent said, "Thank you, Miss Todd."

Raymond turned to face Kent. He said, "I've been a frightful coward, but I'm glad it's over now."

Kent said, "Please sit down."

"No. What I have to say won't take long. After I saw Miss St. Arles I decided to make another effort to talk with my father. I reached home shortly before eleven and found the house dark. I entered the library and put the light on."

Kent leaned forward. I found myself doing the same.

Raymond said, "The furniture was thrown about as you saw it the following morning. There were even some bloodstains on one of the chairs. However, my father's body wasn't in the room nor had any false faces been painted." His face was pale and drawn as though he were seeing again that picture of devastation.

"While I stood, not knowing what to do, the telephone rang. On an impulse I answered it, perhaps because I hoped my father was calling. Instead, it was Miss St. Arles, who took for granted that she was speaking with my father. She claimed to be speaking from Mr. Morgan's place and mentioned an appointment my father had made with him. To get rid of her, I pretended to be my father and agreed to come to Mr. Morgan's later. Almost as soon as I hung up, another call came in. Since I couldn't make matters worse, I answered again. It was Gail. Until now I was sure she had not recognized my voice. As soon as Gail finished, I phoned Miss Todd and acquainted her with the situation. She advised me to leave at once."

He paused. Kent said encouragingly, "Please go on."

"There really isn't any more. I rejoined Miss Todd and we went on to the dinner party. On the way we decided that by continuing the pretense of my father having been home at eleven I was providing an alibi for myself if, as seemed likely, something had happened to him."

"And you determined to strengthen your alibi by claiming to have talked with him yourself."

He hung his head. "Yes. Mr. Morgan's statement that he too had phoned my father was a surprise, but I was in no position to challenge it."

Kent said absently, "We have cleared up Mr. Morgan's share in the deception."

Laura asked timidly, "What are you going to do?"

"For the time being—nothing. I am strongly inclined to believe Mr. Dillon's story, since it coincides with other information we have received." He stood up. "I am grateful for your frankness, tardy though it may be."

Raymond seemed reluctant to leave without an opportunity to justify himself further, but Kent firmly cut short his stammered explanation. When they had finally gone, I said, "I suppose you've been told how I squared Hendrickson and the stuff he gave me about Firelli and O'Connor. We're cooperating with the D.A.—for the time being. We've got to solve these murders now."

Kent sighed, "I should have taken your advice last night. We have played into those scoundrels' hands."

I scoffed. "Your guess was as good as mine. We got a tough break is all. We've survived tough ones before." A new thought struck me. "Why didn't you tell that poor goof his sister was hibernating under Benton's watchful eye?"

Kent said gravely, "I told Mr. Dillon the truth. Benton phoned at eight-thirty to inform me that Miss Dillon had slipped out during the night and had not returned."

I picked up my hat. "I'll play just one hunch. If she's not where I think, I'll be right back. Otherwise I'll phone you."

Kent nodded. He said, "Go if you wish, but I wash my hands of Miss Dillon."

## CHAPTER 17

I PUT my finger on the bell button. The brassy clamor from the kitchen echoed hollowly through the apartment, ceased abruptly as I relaxed my finger. I put my ear to the door, then my lips. I said, "This is Chet. I know you're inside. Will you open up or do I have to kick my way in?"

She must have been flattened against the wall. She said in a muffled voice, "Go away. I hate you."

The door vibrated under my resounding blows. I heard a gasp, then fingers fumbling with the lock. I threw my weight against the panel, caught her off balance and sent her reeling against the wall. She bounced off, a spitting demon.

I sidestepped, letting the force of her rush expend against and slam the door to behind me. She whirled and sprang again, her arms flailing. I ducked, caught her about the waist and lifted her bodily off the floor. Clenched fists beat against my face, but she didn't utter a sound.

I set her down so hard I could feel the jar run up my hands. She snarled savagely and sank to the floor. I carried her inside and dumped her on the bed. She lay still, eyes closed, mouth lax.

I bent down, gripped her shoulders, and drew her to me. She turned her head away. I said with my mouth against her cheek, "You love this. You said so yourself." I put my hand behind her neck, forced her head around and kissed her. She bit my lip.

I flung her away. The blood tasted salty in my mouth. I said, "All right, I asked for it. Now let's cut the comedy and be on our way."

She said slowly, "I don't understand. Why should I go with you?"

"Listen," I said, "I've had a rough night. Come on."

She scrambled to her feet, faced me. "What if I did run away from that stupid, horse-faced woman? I'm not accountable to you or your precious Mr. Kent either. I'll go where I choose and when I choose."

I said patiently, "None of this impresses me. I'm not your judge or jury. Save the histrionics for when you'll need them."

She clutched my arm. "Chet—please don't say such things. I ran away last night, but I didn't do anything. What's happened? Who—"

"Antoine St. Arles. I don't know why I'm telling you this when you probably know it better than I do. Raymond gave the police some kind of a yarn about you leaving the house early this morning. They're bound to discover you were out all night, and when they find you ran out on Benton—draw your own conclusions."

If I hadn't caught her she would have toppled over on her face. She wasn't acting; she was out cold. I put her on the bed, brought water from the kitchen. I bathed her face, lowered her head, raised her feet. After what seemed like hours she came out of it.

I said, "If you're a double-feature killer you've chosen the wrong career. You haven't the constitution for it."

It wasn't much of a joke, but it drew a feeble smile. She said, "What shall I do?"

"If you killed her, your best bet is a good lawyer. If you didn't, for Pete's sake stop wasting time and let me take you to Kent. Tell him where you were and what you did."

She said, "I—I can't. You must believe me, Chet. I had nothing to do with her death. I spent the night here—alone. You'll have to trust me."

I held up my left hand, fingers clenched. I raised my thumb. I said, "One: You knew all about your father's plan to leave town. Two: You're under some kind of obligation to Firelli—probably owe him money on gambling debts. Three: You can't account for any part of the evening before I met you and you won't account for what happened after we left Firelli's joint."

She sat up and put her arms about me.

I said, "It's too late for that now. Four: You had me drugged and even lugged back to your house to provide Osmond with another good suspect."

She whispered, "Father was alive at eleven o'clock. I couldn't have hurt him in any way before I met you."

I said, "Hooey—that was Raymond talking. He spilled the whole works to Kent this morning. You pretended to be fooled by his voice because it suited your purpose. I'll make the rest fast. You knew that St. Arles was about ready to spill her story. You gave Benton the slip. If you didn't kill St. Arles, you tipped off Firelli. You had the opportunity at every turn. As against all this, you ask me to take you on faith. Can you give me one single reason why I should trust you?"

Her head was on my shoulder, her mouth pressed against my coat. "You're my husband."

I laughed. "What's that got to do with—" I stopped suddenly. I said, "No. You're kidding. This is another of your stunts." The cold feeling in my midriff told me it was nothing of the sort. Her arms were still about me, her lips brushing my ear. I shook myself loose.

She said, "I thought you'd realize—you're such a fool. That's why I went home for my bag. I don't need a bagful of clothes to stay here overnight. When you first suggested getting married, I thought you were joking and agreed in the same spirit. It wasn't until we left the Cabana that I realized you were in earnest. I was frightened and unhappy. So—"

"Where's the marriage certificate?"

She pointed to her handbag lying on the dresser. I searched its compartments until I found a folded sheet. I read it rapidly. The marriage had been performed by Stanton A. Duncan, by virtue of the authority vested in him as Justice of the Peace, office and residence, 428 Main Street, Marysville. Witnesses were Henrietta Duncan and Jared Beech. The document appeared genuine.

I asked dully, "When did this happen—before or after we went to your house?"

"Before." She was still sitting where I had left her, on the edge of the bed. "You seemed to know what you were doing. I didn't realize there was anything seriously wrong with you until after we returned and discovered Father's body. I tried to make you understand. You acted as though it were a lark. I threw a few clothes into a bag, then went into Father's room. I suppose I was dazed, but it seemed terribly important to get pajamas and things for you. I still don't know where you found the hat."

"You showed Osmond and Hendrickson the certificate, didn't you? That's what they were checking while I was outside."

"Yes. I told them Mr. Kent would fire you if he found out. Don't you see—I thought you really loved me and that after this was all over maybe—"

I said bitterly, "Of all the prize saps—I should have guessed it."

She whispered, "You're horrible."

"Let's skip the amenities. All you care about is saving your neck. I think this marriage was rigged. I'll never feel any different. I'll tell you what. You haven't shown much to date, but I'll gamble on a few drops of sporting blood in your veins and make a bargain with you. If Kent and I pull you out of this mess, will you agree to a divorce or annulment—whichever is easier—as soon as the shouting dies down?"

She surveyed me through narrowed eyes. "Yes. The sooner the better."

"Now you're talking sense. Go home. Tell them we were married Monday but kept it secret because I was afraid of losing my job. I'll try to steer the cops off you altogether, but if you're questioned about last night, admit you were out and say it was my idea to have you give Benton the slip so that you could join me here. Have you got it?"

"Yes."

She shrugged, got up, adjusted her hair, and put on her hat. I said, "There's one condition to this bargain. Keep away from me. I don't ever want to see you again."

She said with contempt, "Don't worry. You won't."

# CHAPTER 18

I SAID to the bartender, "Two more of the same."
I finished the two ryes, and gathered up my change. I said,
"Where's the telephone, pal?"

He said, "My name is Frank." He pointed out the phone against the far wall.

I said, "Thanks, pal," and made it by dead reckoning. I fed it a coin, dialed Kent's private number.

I said, "The bridegroom speaketh."

He said in despair, "You're not drunk. You can't be—not this early."

I said, "I wish I were. I located the Gail in her Montgomery Street hideout. It seems I married her last Monday night. She showed me the certificate signed by a Marysville Justice of the Peace."

"Married? Impossible."

"Wait, there's more. I made a deal with her, swapping an alibi for last night in return for a divorce. The story is that I persuaded her to shake Benton and meet me at the apartment where I was supposed to join her after we left St. Arles' place, only I didn't show up."

He said, unimpressed, "Meet me outside the City Morgue in twenty minutes."

I blinked at the telephone. "Did you say Morgue?"

"Yes. I'm leaving now to pick up Harold Palmer."

"Do you mean Doc Palmer who writes our Health Hints for Housewives column?"

He said impatiently, "Yes. You're sure you're sober?"

"Oh, I'm sober all right," I assured him. "Just what is Doc supposed to do at the Morgue?"

"Perform an autopsy on Dillon's body."

"That'll be nice. And what about my marriage?"

He said, "Meet me in twenty minutes and no nonsense." He slammed the receiver in my ear.

I left the saloon, stepped into a cigar store and bought half a dozen big black cigars which I put into my vest pocket against the moment when they would be needed. I then took a cab to the City Morgue and hung around outside until Kent and Harold Palmer drove up in Harold's car.

The Morgue attendant looked up as we entered the waiting room, surveying us with cold eyes. Kent pushed me forward.

I said, "How do you do? I'm Chet Phelps from the Free Press." I held out my press card for inspection. "We'd like to look at Jeffrey Dillon's body."

He glanced without interest at the press card, and said, "Sure. What for?"

I took out one of the cigars and shoved it into the extended hand.

"You're in the story. I'll play you up big—custodian of the dead—Charon."

He said, "Not Charon—Brannigan. Timothy Brannigan." He stood up, and asked with sudden suspicion, "Who're these guys?"

"A couple of friends. They've never been inside a morgue before." I looked at the immaculate Kent as though with doubt. "I don't know will they be able to take it."

Timothy laughed. He said, "Okay, come on. But don't get sick on the floor."

Harold spluttered indignantly, but fell silent before Kent's wrathful look. We walked along a dimly lit corridor into a room whose walls were lined with drawer-like compartments. Timothy kept up a running fire of conversation in guide-book fashion about the functionings of the Morgue. When he finally pulled out the drawer labeled "Jeffrey Dillon," it was with the air of a magician performing a notable feat of legerdemain.

Kent whispered, "Get him away."

I nodded, but I was too fascinated by the body to make any immediate move. Dillon, on his slab, bore even less resemblance to anything human than he had on the floor of his library. The face under the battered head was sunken and clean-shaven and had been wiped free of its gooey mask, yet evoked no memory of the man whose picture had filled the pages of every newspaper since his death. Something was wrong with his face, but for the life of me I could not say what.

Kent said in his dry voice, "Do you shave their faces as a rule?"

Then I knew what had struck me as a false note. The Dillon whose pictures I remembered had sported a small close-cropped moustache. No wonder Kent had been taken aback by the smoothly shaven face. I clapped my hand to my mouth, made gargling sounds.

Timothy dragged me outside. In the corridor I mopped my brow, smiling in sickly fashion. I said, "I'm awful sorry. I shouldn't have come down here right after I ate."

Timothy said with sympathy, now that his immaculate floor was no longer endangered, "You never know when it's gonna hit you. Funny it didn't bother them two."

I quivered, and edged further from the door. I said, "Look, let's go outside and catch a smoke. There are a couple of things I want to ask you about for the paper."

He said doubtfully, "What about them?"

"They'll be along in a second. Leave them alone. They'll have something to talk about the rest of their lives."

He let me draw him along the corridor. I pressed another cigar on him. I asked, "How long have you been working here? You must have some wonderful stories. Tell me a few, and maybe I can do a whole feature article about you."

With only occasional questions from me, he held forth for a good fifteen minutes. At the end of that time Kent and Palmer emerged. Timothy stopped his narrative, and said, "You sure took your time."

I said quickly, "Well, we must be going, Tim. I've got enough dope now. If I need any more, I'll drop back by."

Out in the street I inquired, "Well, Doc, did you uncover anything?"

He chortled. "Did I not?" He unlocked the car. "Of course, I shall have to verify my findings, but I am practically certain that death was not due to the reasons previously ascribed."

"You mean he wasn't strangled?"

Kent shook his head. "Mr. Dillon was killed by a needle or other thin instrument inserted into the medulla oblongata."

"What's that?"

Palmer explained. "The medulla oblongata is the lowest part of the brain and is located at the back of the neck, just above the spine. It is a highly vulnerable area of the human body and contains bundles of fibers and nuclei of gray matter."

"But the coroner was sure Dillon was strangled," I objected. "How could he be so far wrong?"

"Very easily, in this case," Palmer said. Now that the danger was over, he was enjoying himself immensely. "Of course," he added generously, "I was aided by the fact that Mr. Kent asked me to work on the assumption that the ascribed cause of death was incorrect. You see, the medulla oblongata controls brain centers which influence respiration, swallowing and other functions. An injury caused by a needle inserted into the medulla oblongata could produce paralysis followed by death under circumstances closely resembling strangulation. If you add the suggestion of strangulation in the form of a wire twisted about the neck after death, it is easy to understand how the autopsy surgeon was misled."

"Did you find the needle?"

Kent sniffed, and Palmer said, "Of course not. The presence of a needle would immediately have been revealed. No, I found only a pinprick in the area mentioned, which is why my diagnosis is not complete. I removed a small area of surface skin and the tendon sheath surrounding the prick—perhaps a square inch—and will have to make microscopic examination of the cells before I can render a final opinion."

I said, "Yes. All the extra violence—shooting and the bashed-in skull—was to distract attention from one little pin-prick at the back of the neck."

"No more so than the false faces. My original theory concerning them was both right and wrong. The grease marks were for the purpose of concealment, as I presumed, but they hid the lack of a factor at the scene, rather than the presence of an additional one. The lack was obviously Dillon's moustache. The only purposeful false face was the one painted on Dillon's own face. All the rest were stage setting calculated, by the sheer weight of horror, to draw attention away from the face of the victim."

"I dislike to trouble you with my petty affairs, Mr. Kent," I reminded, "but there's the matter of my being slightly married to consider."

He smiled thinly. "I have no intention of permitting the marriage to go unchallenged—unless, of course, you so elect. However, I am certain we can get no present satisfaction from Miss Dillon. No, the logical person to quiz is Mr. Firelli."

I said, "Mr. Firelli, eh? You're in great form today. Never mind how I find him, with every cop in town on his trail. Just pretend I've got him. What next?"

Kent said unruffled, "Ask him why Miss Dillon considered it necessary to marry you. He should know, since he provided her with an alibi for the early part of the evening, arranged your meeting and drugged you."

"And of course, he'll drop everything and tell me."

"Not certainly, but in all likelihood—if you locate him. Mr. Firelli's regime is finished, in any case. Whatever tie bound him to Miss Dillon is now of no consequence, since he is being hunted for the murder of Lugoni. I fancy Mr. Firelli will be delighted at the opportunity to strike a blow on his own account."

I said, "Well, so long, then. I'll be seeing you—I hope."

I cut across City hall Square and headed uptown in the general direction of the Club Cabana, as good a starting point as any. A cold, steady rain had begun to fall, not hard yet, but with every promise of turning into a deluge soon. It was a rain that hunted out every dry spot on a man and made him appreciate the virtues of a nice inside job like bank teller or shoe salesman. There wasn't a cab in sight. I wondered how it felt to stop a .45 slug and weighed that against the possible alternative of married life with the Gail. I decided in favor of the slug.

# CHAPTER 19

A BIG PADLOCK SEALED the door of the Club Cabana. I walked around front to the restaurant where Kent and I had dined Monday night, but that was locked too. I went around the corner again, past the Cabana's main entrance, look for a rear door, failed to find one.

Firelli had other places in town—the Rockmore Casino out on New York Avenue, the Yacht Club on the river and others, but it seemed to me that if he were in town at all, the Cabana, built to be a gambling house and therefore proof against surprise attacks, would be his most logical hiding place. Apparently I was wrong.

I moved on down the block, and stepped into the first doorway beyond the Club to light a cigarette. I was soaking wet, even though I had managed to take a taxi part of the way. I lit my cigarette, flipped the dead match into the street and prepared to depart when I heard the wail of a police siren. A cab tore around the corner, skidded momentarily and pulled up in front of my doorway as the noise of the siren grew louder.

Two men tumbled out of the cab. One of them was Firelli, gun in hand, the other Hendrickson. Firelli jerked his companion forward, and the two raced toward me. Firelli, head down and half turned, collided with me in the dark of the doorway.

He said hoarsely, "You damn fool. I could have killed you."

I said, "No. You never saw me. I've got to talk to you."

"Come on then. They'll be here in a second."

He unlocked the hall door and shoved Hendrickson in before him. I followed. The house was a deserted tenement. We ran along a narrow unlighted corridor to the cellar stairs in the rear, and in pitch darkness descended. The street noises were suddenly shut out. We went through a second doorway, then upstairs again, and reached another corridor, this one lighted by a dim red bulb.

The corridor ended in still another door. Firelli rapped on it with his gun butt. There was the sharp click of a bolt, and we were in the Club Cabana's main gambling room.

The man who had admitted us bolted the door and turned to face us. He was short and enormously fat, not heavily muscled like the brutish Osmond, but flabby fat and sloppy. He held an enormous revolver in his left hand. He was dressed in a pair of dungaree pants and a dirty shirt open at the neck—his entire outfit contrasting oddly in my memory with the midnight blue dinner jackets I remembered from my last visit. He was the most bowlegged man I had ever seen. I looked about the darkened room, and saw that it was deserted except for Bowlegs.

Firelli said, "They followed me, Gig."

Bowlegs shoved the gun into his pants band and stood there with his fingers scratching nervously on the barrel. He looked like a pirate—a worried pirate with fear-flecked eyes. He said, "We can't hold them off."

Firelli, grinning, slapped Hendrickson on the back. The little man staggered. Firelli said, "We don't have to hold them off—not for a while anyway. We got their ace in the hole." He took Hendrickson's arm and led him across the room, calling over his shoulder, "Come on, Phelps. You can sit in on the fun."

I followed, conscious of Gig at my heels. We entered a small private office. It held a safe, open and empty, a desk and some chairs. The only object on the desk was a telephone. Firelli pulled chairs over to the dask and sat down behind it.

Color crept back to Hendrickson's face as he finally recognized me. He wailed, "Phelps. Oh God, Phelps. He's going to kill me. Don't let him do it, Phelps." His voice broke in a hysterical moan.

Firelli made a grimace of disgust, got up from his chair, walked around the desk to Hendrickson. His gun dangled from his finger. He leaned over Hendrickson, flipped the gun so that the muzzle rested on his palm, and struck Hendrickson lightly with the butt. The little man fell out of his chair and sprawled on the floor, whimpering. Firelli walked away.

I didn't move. I said, "This isn't like you, Firelli, slugging a helpless man, and the D. A. at that."

I could tell Bowlegs had been hit right where he lived, because he emptied his lungs all at once. He said, "Is that the D.A.?" His eyes darted to Hendrickson, motionless on the floor, then back to me.

"He's nobody else," I confirmed.

Firelli grinned again. He said quietly, "Wait outside, Gig. "There's a sight," he remarked conversationally, "the D.A. crawling on the floor like a dog."

The phone on the desk rang. Firelli exulted, "What did I tell you?" He picked it up. "This is Firelli. Go ahead."

A puzzled frown furrowed his brow. "Who is this calling?" he asked. He listened again, presently said, "The whole two hundred grand? Okay, sure, I'll be there." He hung up and turned to me. He said. "There's a belly laugh for you. Two hundred grand is waiting for me in the Dillon house. All I have to do is to go after it."

I said quickly, "It's a trap. Don't fall for it."

He sighed, poked the gun muzzle under his hat and scratched his head. He said, "Maybe. What the hell difference does it make? I can't bust out of here now." He grinned. "You neither."

I shrugged. "I'll worry about that when the time comes."

"Me, too," Firelli agreed. He laid the gun down on the table. "You got a gall smelling around me after the way you run with them two cut-ups." His eyes glittered.

"I don't run with anybody except Kent, and you know it."

He shook his head. "I want you to look at it my way. A newspaper guy should stay on the sidelines and call them the way he see them. When he mixes in he has to take his chances, same as anybody else."

"There's a lot in what you say," I conceded, and meant it. "But only up to a certain point. When I came here the other night I was looking to lose a little money. I didn't ask to have Gail Dillon wished on me for any of what followed. If I didn't stay on the sidelines it was because you wouldn't let me." I thought of the police outside and said, "What's the sense of arguing? It looks like we'll both get our lumps before long."

Firelli reached into the bottom drawer of the desk, produced another gun and a box of cartridges. He loaded the gun, clicking the barrel shut and open after inserting each shell. His hat was pushed far back on his head. Each time he snapped the gun he jerked his head and the hat quivered. He said finally, "All right. I believe you. But just the same you were crazy to hunt me out today."

"Maybe so," I conceded. "But I'm not far enough gone to pull a stunt like kidnapping the district attorney. You may have had a chance before, but you're as good as on a slab now."

He laughed. "There's lots worse places." He got up, poked Hendrickson with his foot. "Wake up, sweetheart; we got work to do." He turned back to me. "There's a pure yellow bastard for you. I walked right into his office past two cops and a dozen secretaries. You should have seen his face. All he had to do on the way out was holler just once and it would have been all over. But did he? Not a word."

He dragged Hendrickson over to the desk and pushed him into a chair. Hendrickson stared at him with glazed eyes. Firelli took one of the guns from his pocket, winked openly at me and thrust the muzzle against Hendrickson's nose.

"Smell that," he ordered.

Hendrickson recoiled from the metal.

"Do you hear me? I'm going to shove this up your nose and blow your brains out the back of your head if you don't do what I tell you."

"Anything—for God's sake, anything—only don't hit me again," Hendrickson begged.

Firelli spoke heartily. "Now you're talking sense. Call up Osmond and tell him where you are—not that he doesn't know. Tell him the first copper who tries to break in here will find you croaked. Tell him I'll swap you for a fast car, with the motor running. Tell him to park the car right in front of the Cabana and to call off his men. Tell him if they let me blow town Gig will release you unharmed."

Hendrickson dialed the phone with trembling fingers. He got Police Headquarters, asked for Osmond. There was a long silence and a reply I didn't need to hear. The expression of despair on Hendrickson's face told me enough. Hendrickson slowly hung up. Tears streamed down his cheeks.

Firelli said, "The bastard isn't there."

Hendrickson said, "Please, Mr. Firelli. I did my best. Please don't kill me."

The phone rang. Firelli picked it up. A delighted grin spread over his face. He spoke into the mouthpiece. "Sure. He's right here." He turned to Hendrickson. "He's calling from across the street. Tell him like I told you and make it good."

Hendrickson took the telephone which Firelli held so that both could hear Osmond's reply. Hendrickson repeated his instructions, adding an impassioned plea on his own account. Firelli said nothing, but kept nodding his head as Osmond spoke. At last he took the phone from Hendrickson, and said, "All right, Osmond. But don't try no tricks." He hung up.

I said, "Will you answer a few questions for me?"
Firelli turned to me. "What do you want to know?"
"Did you kill Dillon?"
He toyed with his gun, twirling the barrel. It was not meant as a threatening gesture. He said, "No, but if I knew then what I do now I would have."
"What do you know?"
"Dillon drew down over a hundred grand of my money, mostly from the traction fix. That's why the deal fell through, not because of the dirt your paper printed. The right guys never got theirs. They couldn't complain, but they didn't stay right. I couldn't prove anything, but I watched him. He decided to skip, but in a way to make it look like he was kidnaped and murdered. He picked a quarrel with Morgan, too, so that one of us would be sure to take the rap."
"That's the way Kent doped it."
Firelli said, "There's another cute bastard. Anyway, Dillon fixed his act too good. He made a perfect set-up for a murder. Somebody took it over."
"Where was Dillon killed?"
"Not in his own house."
"How do you know?"
"Because I went there after he called Morgan. There was nobody in except his daughter, and the joint was all tossed around. Then Morgan showed up. I didn't want him getting no ideas, so I chased him."
I said, "Then the reason you gave the Dillon kid an alibi was because she had seen you at the house."
"Yes."
"Why did she marry me?"
Firelli stared, then guffawed. "She did? That's a hot one. When I told her to tie on to you for an alibi, I said, kidding-like, it would be perfect if you two got married. I didn't think she'd take me serious."
"You and your ideas."
"She ain't so bad," he said, trying to keep his face straight. "A little wild, but you could do worse."
"Thanks. Why did you send Lugoni to my room for the hat with the M.A.C. initials?"
"I never wanted the hat. I didn't tell you, but I was at Dillon's a second time that night. Around midnight—while you and the Dillon kid were still here—somebody called up and left a message if I wanted to find Dillon he was at home. I went up there and found him all right, but he was dead."

"Complete with false faces?"

"Yes. Not the first time, but then. The first time only the library was tore up the way he planted it. Anyway, about the hat. I was hunting those phony papers Dillon mentioned to Morgan—I didn't know about the money until the next day. I looked upstairs in Dillon's room and seen his hat. Then in the morning at Kent's office you had the hat. Remember? I knew then you must have been to Dillon's joint after me and maybe you found the papers or the money. So I sent Lugoni out to frisk your room."

"One thing more," I asked. "Why was I drugged?"

He gestured vaguely. "You certainly gave me trouble. First you didn't fall for the Dillon kid, so I had to fix up that phony fight. Then later you got to worrying about it and the way you were winning." He grinned at the memory. "You certainly are one stubborn guy. The wheel was on the level, but you wouldn't believe it. You wanted to leave without your winnings or the girl. I couldn't let you do that. Catching me at the house, she had me over a barrel. So—" He shrugged. "It was a plain Mickey Finn. Guys get it every day, but it must have hit you extra hard."

Gig waddled in. He said, "A dick just parked a heap in front of the door and beat it."

Firelli stood up. He said tersely, "That's it." He turned to Hendrickson, who had been listening in silence. "Up, you."

Hendrickson wabbled erect. He asked fearfully, "What are you going to do? You promised—"

Firelli smiled. "There's a car out front. Osmond left it just like he promised. You don't think he'd pull any fast ones, do you?"

Hendrickson babbled, "No, no. He assured me."

"Then that's fine. I'm handing you a break you wouldn't give me. All you got to do is put on my hat and coat, go out there and drive the crate away."

Gig said, "Boss, you're crazy. He wouldn't cross us."

Firelli snarled, "Shut up, Gig." He took off his coat, stripped Hendrickson's raincoat from his back and forced the exchange. He said harshly, "On your way. The rest is strictly between you and your pal."

I raised my voice in protest. "You can't do this, Firelli. You knew it was a trap all along."

"Keep quiet, Phelps."

He took the ashen Hendrickson by the arm and dragged him outside.

From the street there came a fusillade of shots and the abrupt staccato cough of a machine gun, then silence. Firelli appeared in the doorway.

He said with relish, "Well, that's the end of—"

Gig had no heroic size image of himself in his mind. He raised his gun and shot Firelli twice at point blank range. Firelli leaned against the doorway. He said, "Gig—" He fell forward on his face. Gig spat. "The crazy fool," he said. "He was a mad dog."

I grabbed the phone.

## CHAPTER 20

I PICKED UP KENT in front of the Free Press building. Raymond Dillon was with him. They piled into my taxi, and Kent gave the driver the address of the Dillon house, adding, "Hurry!" He turned to me. "You aren't hurt?"

"No. The only real danger was when they came in. Gig yelled out that Firelli was dead, but I was afraid some nervous cop would let go a blast anyway."

Our cab passed a light and narrowly avoided collision with a station wagon. Raymond jumped. He said, "Need we risk our lives? I tell you I phoned the house a half hour ago and there was no answer." He threw me a covert look. "Are you sure—"

I said violently, "Rollo, you get in my hair. I don't know the ethics of slugging a brother-in-law, but—"

"That will do, Chet." Kent placed a restraining hand on my arm. He leaned forward, urged the driver to greater speed. "If anything has happened I will never forgive myself. I should have realized immediately—" He subsided, muttering.

Mostly to keep up my courage, I explained, "I only heard one side of the conversation. Maybe whoever found the money felt it belonged to Firelli and meant only to turn it over to him."

Kent said, "I hope so." His mouth was the familiar thin line. "Why did you come downtown, Mr. Dillon? When you phoned, I expressly ordered you to go home and remain there until I was in communication with Chet again."

I asked Raymond, "Where did you call from?"

"The University Club. Gail and I had lunched there. She wanted me to prepare Mother for the news of her marriage, but at the last moment decided to do it herself. I wasn't satisfied with her story and called Mr. Kent after she left."

Kent said, "It is now almost four-thirty. You did not go home as I asked. How did you spend the time after leaving your sister?"

Angry spots of color appeared in his cheeks. "If you are insinuating that it was I who called Firelli—"

"Oh, for heaven's sake," Kent snapped. "Will you answer my questions without this eternal arguing?" Evidently his own nerves were in none too good a shape.

Raymond said more quietly, "It was well after two when I first phoned you. I wanted to discuss this marriage with Laura, but when ·I called I was told she was visiting my mother. That's why I didn't go home. It seemed wiser to let the three women talk things out by themselves. I remained at the Club for a while and then came downtown in the hope of learning the truth about this marriage. You were busy, Mr. Kent, and couldn't see me at once. While I waited, I rang up the house but got no answer."

Kent sighed, cutting off further explanations with a wave of his hand.

I said, "We're almost there. Maybe we'll find it was only a false alarm."

Kent nodded absently, and we fell silent until the cab pulled up before the Dillon house. I was out first, with Raymond right behind me. Kent lingered a moment to pay the driver.

I almost tripped over the Gail as we pushed open the door. She lay just inside the dark vestibule, her golden hair spilled loosely over the floor. There was an ugly lump behind her left ear. She had evidently been hit while removing her coat and had fallen partly over it.

Kent ran up the stairs and ordered sharply, "Don't stand there gaping. Pick her up."

I came out of my daze, gathered her in my arms and carried her to a couch in the anteroom while Kent and Raymond hastened upstairs. I made a quick examination of the Gail's neck and skull. Nothing seemed broken, and she was breathing.

I hunted about, found glasses and a decanter of what smelled like bourbon in a cabinet. I raised the Gail's head, moistened her lips with a few drops of liquor, chafed her wrists. Her eyelids fluttered, opened wide. I held the glass to her lips. She pushed it away, stared at me for a moment, moaned and closed her eyes again.

I forced the liquor between her lips, whispering, "Come on, soldier; snap out of it. It's me, Chet. You're safe now."

She trembled, flung her arms around my neck, and pressed her lips fiercely against mine. There was a sound of running feet, and

Raymond burst in. He leaned against the doorway, looking as though he were about to be sick. He said weakly, "Phelps—" He swayed and suddenly collapsed.

I removed the Gail's arms from about my neck, shouted, "Stay here," and dashed out. I met Kent at the foot of the stairs.

He said somberly, "No need to hurry," and led the way upstairs to one of the bedrooms, indicating the .open door. He said quietly, "We're too late."

Veronica was on the bed. She had been tied and gagged with strips of what appeared to be a bedsheet, then shot through the heart. On the floor, not far from the bed, Laura Todd lay in a crumpled heap.

I pushed Kent aside, bent over Laura, and saw at once she hadn't been shot. There was nothing to be done for Veronica, but Kent had been wrong in supposing Laura dead, too. He watched me pick her up. "For God's sake, do something," I implored.

He said, "Take her into the living room." He made no move to help me, but went downstairs again. I carried Laura into an adjoining bedroom and tried to revive her. She was still unconscious when Kent returned with Raymond and the Gail. Raymond sank into a chair and covered his face with his hands. The Gail tottered over to me and tried to help with Laura.

I said to Kent, "Have you called the police?"

He nodded, watched me work over Laura. She stirred but did not open her eyes. Quiet footsteps sounded on the stairs. I motioned for silence, picked up a heavy piece of bric-a-brac and tiptoed out into the hall. When I recognized Morgan I lowered my weapon.

Kent said, "Come up, by all means. You may be able to cast some light on the murder of Mrs. Dillon."

Morgan said stupidly, "Murder—Mrs. Dillon?" Fear sprang into his eyes. He suddenly pushed by us and went swiftly down the hall to Veronica's bedroom, where he stood in the doorway.

"I warned her," he said wearily. He turned away. "I suppose the police have been notified?"

Kent said, "Yes. I called state police a moment ago."

"State police?" Morgan looked puzzled.

The front door banged, and there was a scuffling of many feet. Kent said, "I fancy they have arrived." He left us, and descended the stairs swiftly. Morgan and I went into the bedroom where Laura was still lying on the bed with the Gail bent over her. Raymond had not changed his position of shocked helplessness.

Kent came back with a lieutenant of state police, two troopers and a prisoner. I looked up in surprise as I recognized the man's bruised face.

Kent noted my expression. "You know this man?"

I said, "Sure. He's George Lynn Collins—Osmond's clay pigeon. Where did you find him?"

One of the troopers answered, "He was loitering near the corner."

Collins said frantically, "I was waiting for Mrs. Dillon."

Kent smiled grimly. I said, "You'll have a long wait, Mister."

Collins gazed wildly about, read confirmation in the rings of faces. On the couch Laura opened her eyes and suddenly sat up. She whispered, bewildered, "Where am I?"

Kent soothed her. "You are in no danger, Miss Todd." He looked from her to Raymond, who had not raised his head at the sound of her voice. Kent continued, "You were attacked by the same person who shot Mrs. Dillon. Can you tell us anything about it?"

Laura looked from Kent to Raymond and back again. She said faintly, "I—it was all so sudden. Veronica and I were in the bedroom. A man came in—" Her voice died away.

Kent encouraged, "A smallish dark man with black hair?"

She nodded. "Yes." She passed her hands over her eyes. "I saw him once before. I—I think it was Mr. Firelli. He demanded the money he insisted Veronica was hiding and—"

Kent said, "That will do, Miss Todd. Firelli is dead."

She sighed, and said simply, "I'm so glad."

Kent answered politely, "I don't doubt it." He spoke under his breath to the police lieutenant, who walked over to Laura's side. Kent said, "Laura Todd, I accuse you of the murders of Jeffrey Dillion, Antoine St. Arles and Veronica Dillon." The police lieutenant put his hand on her shoulder.

She made no effort to resist. She said, "I don't understand. Raymond—"

Kent said, "I'm afraid your fiancé has already guessed at your guilt. It is futile to accuse Firelli, Miss Todd. Chet was with him when you made your last, fruitless attempt to shift your guilt. Mr. Firelli did not keep his appointment to be killed because at the moment you called he was being besieged by the police."

Laura said, "I don't know what you're talking about."

"It's no use, Miss Todd," Kent said. "As soon as I discovered the reason for the false faces and the manner in which Jeffrey Dillion died, it was not difficult to trace his movements. We have already located a porter who remembers the smooth-shaven gentleman who suffered what appeared to be a heart attack in Union Terminal and who helped his pretty niece carry him out to her car. There must have been other witnesses as well who will step forward when the incident is properly publicized."

Laura said, "What has this to do with me?"

"Everything, and for the best possible reason. Your hatred of Jeffrey Dillion was only exceeded by his contempt for you. He knew why you wanted to marry his weakling son—for money with which to bolster your social position. And because you are clever, you knew he knew."

Laura murmured, "Really, Mr. Kent, this is fantastic."

Kent pounced. "You will find it increasingly so. When the senior Dillon abruptly ceased opposing his son's engagement, you were not taken in. You watched and kept your own counsel. You alone correctly interpreted the reason why he had goaded his own son into apparently betraying him. Later, you encouraged the reconciliation between father and son because it was necessary for you to have free entry into Dillon's home.

"Given the first clue, it must have been easy enough to discover the disappearance plan, as others also discovered it. Probably, toward the end, Jeffrey had actually some of the unbalance he fancied he was pretending. You followed him or his daughter to the Montgomery Street hideaway and bit by bit pieced together the plan. You may even have eavesdropped on their conversations.

"Your own scheme was in readiness. You determined to kill Jeffrey Dillon, but it was your intention to wait until the stage set of his mock murder had been fully prepared. At that moment you needed only to appear, shoot him, and the blame would inevitably be placed where your victim had himself directed—on Firelli or Morgan.

"Instead, Mr. Dillon advanced his departure by a day. The opportunity to kill him in his own home was lost and, indeed, he almost escaped you altogether. Your suspicions were aroused when you learned, almost too late, that he was alone in the house Monday night. Through skillful suggestion you persuaded Raymond to visit Miss St. Arles. As soon as he left, you hastened in your car to Union Terminal, intercepted Dillon. You threw your arms about him in what appeared to be a farewell kiss. It was quite literally a kiss of death. You plunged a needle or perhaps a short hatpin into his brain. Dillon collapsed in your arms, not yet dead but utterly paralyzed. With the help of a porter, you carried him out to your car."

Laura met his gaze without flinching.

"Still unconvinced?" Kent asked. He shook his head in pity. "You have been very unlucky, Miss Todd. From your first move until your final attempt to provide a scapegoat in the person of the equally ill-starred Mr. Firelli, misfortune dogged your footsteps. Your impromptu method of killing required mutilation of the body, a task which must have shaken even you. The discovery that Jeffrey had shaved his moustache created the need for the false faces, a risky device—yet unavoidable. Many people must have witnessed the comedy at Union Terminal. If, the next day, it had been found that the murdered man had shaved off his moustache shortly before he died, much would have been made of that fact. Pictures.of Jeffrey Dillon with and without his moustache would have been prominently displayed in all the papers. Inevitably the porter who had helped you, or a casual witness to the scene, would have recognized Dillon for the man who had fallen ill at the station. Unquestionably, you painted the false faces with grease taken from the family car parked in the garage, a source theoretically accessible to any prowler. As it developed, you ran no risk, since the police laboratory was unable to differentiate between the grease from the various cars tested.

"Your bad luck persisted when Miss St. Arles phoned here just as Raymond arrived, because, of course, she immediately saw through his masquerade. You had not counted upon that. You sent Raymond to see his father in order that—"

She said viciously, "All right. You caught me. But he," she pointed to Raymond, "put me up to it. It was his idea. He wanted me to kill his father so that we could have the money he was planning to run away with."

Raymond's eyes bulged. He was incapable of speech.

"No," Kent replied. "I know what you hope to achieve. This is your last move, but it comes too late. You seek to involve your fiancé in the hope that the missing funds which must soon be found will be used in your joint defense. Really, for one so far-sighted you deserved better luck." He turned away.

The lieutenant nodded to his men. Still struggling, Laura was carried off. There was a moment of stunned silence. Collins was the first to speak. "May I go now?"

Kent's lip curled. He said emphatically, "No, sir, you may not. Consider yourself lucky that you are not facing a murder charge for the second time. When did you and Mrs. Dillon plan this mock hold-up?"

"It was Veronica's idea," Collins broke down. "She came to see me this afternoon and told me her son's fiancée had found the money. She made me tie her up while there was nobody in the house so that she could pretend there had been a robbery."

Morgan spoke for the first time. He said, "I feared this tragedy. I long ago discarded the theory of missing papers and became convinced that Jeffrey's money was hidden in the house."

"Yet you told us the fiction of missing papers as though you believed it."

Morgan shrugged. "My first duty was to my clients." He avoided Kent's eyes. "I warned Mrs. Dillon that the probable presence of so much money in the house constituted a danger."

Kent gave him a skeptical look. "We have no way of proving otherwise, but for your own conscience's sake I hope you are right. Otherwise you share at least moral responsibility for Mrs. Dillon's death."

Morgan was indignant. "I do not follow your reasoning."

"I shall be happy to explain. Miss Todd came here some time this morning and found the missing money for Mrs. Dillon—a simple matter, since she herself had hidden it. Afterward she pretended to leave, confident that Mrs. Dillon's greed would never permit sharing the discovery with her children. Mrs. Dillon communicated with her paramour, Mr. Collins, and between them they simulated a robbery, to all of whose details Miss Todd was unquestionably a hidden observer."

The downstairs door banged and another contingent of state troopers came upstairs. They went down the hall to Veronica's bedroom. The Gail made as though to leave. The police lieutenant shook his head. "You'll all have to stay here," he ordered. The Gail sat down again, weeping silently.

Kent paid no attention to the byplay. He concentrated on the increasingly uncomfortable lawyer. "Collins bound Mrs. Dillon, then left to await word of the scheme's success. Miss Todd now emerged from her hiding place and telephoned Firelli, her intention being to shoot him when he arrived and then kill the helplessly bound woman, thus simultaneously eliminating a claimant for the money and catching Firelli, whom the police were already seeking for Lugoni's murder.

"But Miss Todd's ill fortune still pursued her. Firelli did not arrive. Time grew short. Miss Dillon arrived and was struck down. Miss Todd was now faced with the alternative of killing Mrs. Dillon or permitting the pseudo-robbery to go unchallenged. She elected to kill her fiancé's mother, secured the money from the hiding place of Mrs. Dillon's selection and cached it as before, probably along with the gun which she must have purchased when she first decided to kill Jeffrey Dillion."

Morgan kept his eyes on the ground. He said presently, "I advised Mrs. Dillon to the best of my ability and in all sincerity."

"I hope so." Kent addressed Raymond. "When did you first suspect Miss Todd's guilt?"

Raymond said brokenly, "This morning—when I learned of Miss St. Arles' death." A quiver passed through his frame. "I tried to dismiss it from my mind, but I could not help recalling how strangely Laura acted last night right after she received a phone call. I thought nothing of it at the time, though I wondered why only a few minutes later she invented what sounded like an excuse to send me home."

Kent said, "That must have been Miss St. Arles. Undoubtedly she confronted your fiancée with her knowledge of your impersonation, which she must have considered ample proof of your guilt. I imagine Miss St. Arles told your fiancée of my willingness to pay five thousand dollars for this information. We can only conjecture what happened thereafter. In all likelihood Miss Todd pretended to be terror-stricken and convinced the would-be blackmailer of her willingness to pay a greater price for her silence. She learned that Miss St. Arles was at home and alone, and acted with characteristic swiftness." Kent stopped, reluctant to reveal his share in what had followed. He veered away from danger. "Surely, Mr. Dillon, your suspicions had greater foundation than mere concern over an unknown telephone call."

Raymond nodded slowly. "I told you in the taxi that I tried to reach Laura this afternoon. Mrs. Todd mentioned that Gail had called me there last night only a few minutes after I left. But when I spoke to Laura this morning she said nothing of Gail's call."

"Yet you knowingly permitted her to be alone with your mother and sister even after I warned you as best I could?"

Raymond said miserably, "It was only a suspicion—too horrible —" His face contorted with pain.

The Gail moved over beside me and took my hand. She said, "I'm sorry, Chet."

"I never really thought you had any share in it," I lied.

She moved closer. "I love you, Chet. Truly I do."

I sagged against the side of the couch in my best morgue-sick manner, groaning hollowly. Kent shouted, "Chet—what's the matter?"

I clutched at his sleeve. "I need a doctor," I moaned.

"Is it that serious?"

I screwed up my features, opened my mouth, and rolled my eyes. The Gail screamed. Kent took one horrified look, cried, "Oh, my God," and practically dragged me out.

# CHAPTER 21

KENT SAID in a voice tinged with apprehension, "Keep that shade drawn."

I said, "Aw, what's biting you? We're going through the freight yards now. Do you think she'd chase us on a hand-car?"

We made our way to the combination club car and bar, sat down at one of the little tables. Kent ordered Scotch and soda.

I said, "Something tells me we better keep out of the state for a while. I don't want anybody raising questions about robbing graves or fooling with dead bodies."

Kent said fervently, "I concur."

I yawned, and sipped the drink the waiter set before me. I said, "And another thing. How did you happen to pick on Union Terminal as the scene of Dillon's murder, and when did you have a chance to find the porter who helped Todd lug the old boy out to her car?"

Kent laughed. "Guesswork, I must confess. A man who seeks to disappear inconspicuously is unlikely to use an automobile or any form of unusual transportation. Hence Union Terminal. As for the porter—there had to be one. Miss Todd is too clever not to have realized the risk attending aid from a casual passerby who might prove over-solicitous and on whom the incident would make a lasting impression. A porter performs his service, accepts his tip and thinks no more of it."

A familiar voice at my elbow said, "How would you gents like to make up a rubber of bridge?"

I looked up into the grinning face of Jerry. Behind him stood Roy, sardonic and amused as always.

"Hello, boys," I said. I turned to Kent. "Mr. Kent, I want you to meet a couple of pals, Jerry Candle and Roy Meade."

They sat down, Roy beside Kent, Jerry on my side of the table. Roy gave the waiter his order for two rye highballs and bridge cards. He took a folded copy of the Free Press from his pocket and passed it across the table to me. He said, "Been reading the papers lately, pal?"

I opened the paper and glanced at the headlines. The solution to the false face murders was almost lost in the blazing headlines announcing the death of Firelli and District Attorney Hendrickson as eye-witnessed by a Free Press reporter. The lead article, under my byline, and of which I had written not one word, set forth a detailed account of Firelli's Last Stand, including the kidnapping of Hendrickson—which in some miraculous fashion I was supposed to have observed—the phone call to Osmond, the death of Hendrickson through Osmond's treachery, and finally the murder of Firelli by the last of his henchmen. In the left-hand column I read that the Governor had suspended the city administration pending an investigation of its corrupt law enforcement officials.

The waiter came with their drinks and the cards. Roy broke the seal on one deck, shuffled the cards.

Kent asked, "What—ah—stakes shall we play?"

Roy said, "Whatever you say. How about a penny a point?"

Kent turned pale. I said, "Mr. Kent doesn't play high stakes. It's bad for his heart. Make it a twentieth."

Jerry said amiably, "Okay, a twentieth."

Roy said, "One diamond. Where's your wife, pal?"

Kent said, "Pass."

Jerry said, "A heart."

I said, "One spade. How do you know I'm married?"

Jerry groaned, "What are we gonna do, play bridge or gab?"

Roy said, "Shut up. Two hearts. We was with you when you got married."

Kent said, "Well, well. Double two hearts."

"What system is that from?" I queried.

Kent said with dignity, "It merely means that while I cannot support a spade bid or stop game in hearts, I can nevertheless—"

Jerry folded his cards. "Listen, pal, wouldn't it be easier just to put your hand on the table and let him look for hisself?"

Roy said, "Shut up. The guy don't play much bridge. Let him explain."

I waved it aside. "Never mind. I get the idea."

Jerry said bitterly, "Four hearts and cut out the gab."

I said, "Double." Kent threw me a withering look. Roy redoubled and Jerry made the bid with an overtrick. He felt better after that. While Kent shuffled, Jerry stated, "Sure we was with you. Don't you remember?"

"No."

Kent said, "One club."

Jerry said, "One diamond."

"Hey," I protested. "That's my bid." I inspected my cards. "How did you happen to be along?"

Roy put down his cards. He said, "Look, let's get this out of the way and then we can maybe have a decent game."

Kent said, "Merely to satisfy my curiosity, Mr. Meade, would you mind answering a few questions?"

Roy said, "Sure. Anything."

"You knew, did you not, that Mr. Dillon intended to disappear last Monday night?"

Roy grinned. "Yes."

Kent said, "Thank you very much. I could not reconcile your presence with coincidence. In that case, your informant could only have been Mr. Collins."

Roy nodded. He said, "Yes. Collins. We found out about the money he stole from his firm and the way he was hanging around Dillon's wife. After that it was a cinch to get the dope from him."

Jerry frowned. "Is this smart?"

Roy said, "What's the difference? We didn't hurt nobody. And we're queered for life in that town. I want to see is this guy as smart as I heard around."

Kent practically simpered. He said: "I appear to have a reputation. Let me endeavor to live up to it. Would you like me to reconstruct your share in the events of last Monday night?"

"Go as far as you like," Roy said.

"Very well. I think perhaps I had best begin by saying that I never for a moment suspected you or Mr. Firelli of any share in the actual murder."

Jerry asked, interested, "Why not?"

"Toward the last, Jeffrey Dillon became assailed by the fear that his plan was in danger of being discovered, perhaps through the actions of his daughter, who sincerely believed she was aiding her father to escape from deadly enemies. He therefore advanced the date of his departure without letting even her know of the changed schedule. At nine-thirty Monday night he sent her to the Montgomery Street apartment on some trumped-up errand and, while she was gone, set the machinery of his disappearance into operation."

Roy demanded, "Where do we come in?"

"Until a few hours ago I had no idea. I think I can now hazard a good guess. Acting on information received from Mr. Collins, you were in town studying the weak spots in Mr. Firelli's organization, probably with a view to putting pressure on Dillon. Although we have not been able to prove it, I am reasonably certain that on the fatal night Mrs. Dillon had arranged to meet Collins, with whom she was conducting a clandestine affair."

Jerry said, "What's that last mean?"

Roy said, "Shut up. I'll explain later."

"Collins, his suspicions aroused by something Mrs. Dillon told him, communicated with you. You hastened to the Dillon house, only to find the quarry flown. Concerning what follows I can only surmise. I think you remained in the vicinity long enough to observe Miss Dillon return and noted the subsequent arrival of Firelli and Morgan a few minutes apart. In order to keep Firelli under continued observation, you went to the Club Cabana and satisfied yourself that he intended to remain there.

"You left the Cabana after having talked with Chet and reestablished communication with Collins, probably instructed him to keep Mrs. Dillon out as late as possible. One of you then returned to the Dillon house while the other kept watch over the Cabana. Let us say that you, Mr. Candle, were delegated to make the trip uptown."

Jerry laughed. "Okay by me."

"Very well. You arrived to find Dillon's body, but too late to intercept his murderer. You hastened back and informed your colleague of your discovery. While Mr. Meade continued to watch the club, you departed briefly to phone Firelli some ambiguous message to the effect that if he wished to see Dillon he could now do so at the Dillon home. In the meanwhile, Mr. Meade at the club saw Miss Dillon emerge with Chet and engage them in conversation until you returned. Inquiry revealed her intention to go home, which you could not permit—not yet. Flustered, Miss Dillon mentioned the plan earlier suggested to her in jest by Firelli—namely, marriage to Chet. You insisted on taking her out to Marysville, both of you, thus at once keeping her out of the way and also providing yourselves with an alibi in the event of necessity."

Roy said, "No good. How would we know Firelli went back to Dillon's?"

"You knew perfectly well Firelli would act on your message. For your purpose it was sufficient that Firelli's men should know he was stalking Dillon. When the nature of the murder came out, Firelli would be marked a cruel and irresponsible killer in the eyes of his followers. Once the disintegration of his organization began, it would not be difficult to induce a turncoat—say Jack Lugoni—to swear that Firelli went to the Dillon house about midnight and in response to a phone call. You, Mr. Meade, are of a subtle turn of mind. That Firelli ultimately realized his danger is proved by the sudden end of Lugoni.

"Your own plans were slightly endangered through the fears of Mr. Collins, who, after escorting Mrs. Dillon home at one in the morning, returned to the residence. His purpose, I assume, was to obtain the banquet picture which might direct police suspicion at him if, as he suspected, Dillon had carried out his disappearance plan. His indiscretion cost Mr. Collins heavily."

Roy, smiling, conceded, "Not bad. In fact, it's pretty good. What about it?"

It was Kent's turn to smile. He said, "Nothing. I have no grievance against you. You defeated Firelli, but he in turn defeated you. The tragic death of Mr. Hendrickson will remain long in public memory as a reminder of what may be expected of corrupt officials. As witness your presence on this train."

Jerry yawned. "Big words give me a headache. Let's play bridge."

I inquired, "Why did Todd tell Veronica about the hidden money? Why didn't she just keep quiet about it?"

Kent said, "You have evidently never 'found' two hundred thousand dollars. Miss Todd intended to marry Raymond and take her place a a respected member of the community. Her limited financial status was well known. For such a person suddenly to come into possession of a great deal of money would have been a fatal error. She had a much better plan—to have the money found and Veronica eliminated at a single stroke. Undoubtedly the disposal of Miss Dillon at some not too distant date had also been considered."

I said, "Ugh. On the whole I prefer Mrs. Terwilliger."

Roy said, "What I want to know is how you licked the business with the false faces."

Kent expounded. "Concerning the false faces and the mutilations, I was confronted with a choice of premises. If they were independent, I had two murderers to seek, one with reason to paint the false faces, the other to mutilate the body. I rejected this as coincidence beyond probability. But if they were combined, then for what purpose? The reason that immediately suggested itself was identification. Do you follow me?"

Jerry said, "No."

Roy said, "Go ahead."

"But identification of what? Surely not the corpse, since it had been established at Dillon's beyond doubt. I could proceed no further until we had eliminated from consideration the vexing phone calls which appeared to establish Dillon as alive at eleven o'clock. Once it became obvious that he had been dead at that hour—hence had been killed at some place remote from his home and brought back—the puzzle began to assume shape. The killer's purpose could then only be to conceal the fact that Dillon had ever left his home."

Roy said, "It's a little too fast for me, pal. Where does this identification come in?"

"There are many forms of identity. In this case, Miss Todd's problem was to destroy the identity Dillon had created for himself." He turned to me. "Do you recall the tweeds, the new shirt, tie, hat and pajamas? Miss Todd replaced in Dillon's dresser all these incidental items without taking any account of their newness. They provided me with the initial and most important clue. But if new clothes, why not also a new personality? And what easier personality change suggests itself than the removal of one's moustache?"

Jerry said, interested despite himself, "He shaved off his moustache? What do you know about that?"

I said, "Don't tell me you narrowed it down that fine. I don't believe it, no matter how many words you use."

Kent coughed. "As a matter of fact," he confessed, "I went to the Morgue fully prepared to find evidences of plastic surgery, fantastic as it may now seem. Plastic surgery does not alter fingerprints, but can change features so much that it might have been necessary for Miss Todd to mask them. As for the mutilation of the body, I take no credit on that score. Harold determined the reason for it in his examination."

Roy dealt the cards again. "What's this about a needle in the what-do-you-call it?"

I explained. Kent said, "Not a needle. I imagine she used a hatpin."

Jerry sorted his hand. "The whole thing's disgusting, I'll be damned if it ain't. I never did trust dames."

www.ingramcontent.com/pod-product-compliance
Lightning Source LLC
Chambersburg PA
CBHW032156190626
46808CB00021B/1239